# From Submission to Dominance

## A journey of obsession and sexual deviation

**Alex Rissini**

ISBN: 9781672208901

# Part 1 – CHANCE MEETING AND FIRST SEX

# 1

*~ ~ ~ ~ April ~ ~ ~ ~*

If I ever had a dog, it would be big and aggressive, and make people nervous, but it would love me and obey me. Grant's a bit like that dog.

"Grant, can I feel your muscles?"

He laughed. "Feel whatever you want."

He stood up in front of me with his hands on his hips and tensed his body, like in one of those body builder competitions. His arms and legs were bulging, and his chest so powerful. And his swimming shorts were quite revealing.

I stood in front of him, and reached out to his arms, feeling the muscles. "You must be very strong."

I touched his chest, but he made the muscle twitch, and I jumped back.

I scowled at him at first, but then we both started laughing.

He hugged me. "You're good fun, April."

He lifted me up, as if I was no weight at all, and held me there, with my face almost touching his.

For a few moments, we were looking at each other, and I thought he was going to kiss me. It would have been nice, but I'm glad he didn't. I don't like men to assume that they can do what they want. If you let them do something without permission, there's no saying what they might do next. And I couldn't possibly stop him physically.

That's why men need to understand from the start what they're allowed to do. And all men are the same, well at least those worth bothering with. Strong and powerful, but respectful of someone stronger. And that's the woman's role. Not physically stronger, but stronger in purpose, and with a determination to be in control.

## ~ ~ ~ ~ *Grant* ~ ~ ~ ~

It's been a good vacation so far. I'd hitched up with one girl, and bedded her a couple of times. Then she went back home, and left me bored for the last few days. But now I've met April. Sweet little thing. There might be a chance of some intimacy, but she seems so quiet, and meek. She might even be a virgin. Not that I'd hold that against her. We'd met her and her sister by the pool this afternoon, and got on well, and now Harry and I were getting ready for the evening.

"So Harry, how are you getting on with Dawn?"

"Better than you can imagine. I fucked her already, Grant. Not long after we left you and April by the pool."

"How the hell did you manage that?"

"Not me, Grant. It was her idea. Up to her room, and then she started kissing me, and pulling at my clothes, and, well you know."

"You lucky bastard. I'm on a slower track with April. And not that sure we'll get anywhere."

"Well, if she's at all like her sister, you hang in there. From what I saw, April's fascinated with your body, so she's sure to want to share a bed with it. Maybe you'll get lucky tonight."

I laughed. "My body's something all the girls go for. But April's a funny girl. She seems to want to tease me. Touching me, but then if I make any sort of move, backing off. And the hell of it is, she's so sweet and timid, but sometimes she looks at me like my school teacher, as if she's watching for me to do something wrong."

Harry said, "There are other girls you know, and you've only a few days. If you don't think you can screw April, maybe you should move on."

"I'll see how it goes this evening. The crazy thing is I might stay with her, even if she doesn't come across. She's kind of special. You've got to agree to that."

"Yes, if special means weird. Anyway, she's not the sort of girl I'd want. I'll stick with Dawn. God only knows what she'll get up to tonight."

# 2

It's been such fun over the last few days since I met Grant, and Dawn's had a good time too. But we go home soon, and I don't want the vacation to end.

"Dawn, I know it's not been long, but I think I'm falling in love with Grant."

"He's quite a man, so I'm not surprised. But he's a bit big for you isn't he? Does it make you feel protected or something, having him around?"

"Yes, but that's not the most important thing. I enjoy having him with me, and walking along with him, with other people watching us. It's nice knowing he's mine."

Dawn laughed. "Like owning a prize bull?"

"You're joking, but I suppose it's similar to that. He's so strong and powerful, yet if I want something, he jumps to it."

"That's the way men should be. That's what I love about being married to Robin. He does what he's told."

"I had a funny dream last night about Grant and me. It was really peculiar."

Dawn's eyebrows went up. "I know about dreams. Tell me what happened, and I'll tell you what it means."

"Well, it was a circus. I was in the middle of the ring, wearing black underwear, high heels, and a top hat. And I had this long whip. And —"

Dawn laughed. "You didn't bring your black underwear —"

"So what? I don't have a whip either. Anyway, as I was saying, parading around the ring were men, absolutely naked. And Grant was one of them. I shouted that they should start running, and cracked the whip. But they ignored me, so I started hitting them with the tip of the whip, and making them run faster. In the end they were all fallen down with exhaustion, except Grant."

"Is that it?"

"I told him to stop, and I started whipping him, until he fell to his knees. Then I went over to him, and kissed him. And then I woke up."

"That's one weird dream."

"So what does it mean?"

Dawn shrugged. "The heck I know. But if it means you're getting tired of Grant, I'll take him on for you."

"I'll bet you would. But how are you getting on with Harry?"

"We've had so much sex, I'm beginning to lose count. But after all, it's what I came for."

"Really, you shouldn't be doing it, should you? What about Robin?"

"What he doesn't know won't hurt him. Anyway, he must realize I've had sex with other men, and he never says anything, so I don't think he minds."

"Well, it's not the way I'd want a marriage. I'd stay faithful."

"Believe me, it's different once you're married. You'll see. Anyway, what's this about marriage? Are you lining Grant up?"

"Maybe. He's really affectionate. And I enjoy being with him. I really could marry him you know."

"I don't know how you can say that before you've had sex. He might be hopeless in bed."

"He wanted to have sex that first evening. He invited me to his room, and we sat on the bed, talking. Then he told me he loved me, and started kissing me. That was all right, but it was so obvious what he was up to. He put his hand on my breast, and was feeling the shape of it. His hand is so large, … I would have stopped him, but I do like to feel I'm desirable."

"April, you don't need men to grope you to know that. You've a perfect complexion, lovely figure, and you could still pass for a teenager."

"All the same, I like the attention. But then he was at the back of my skirt, to undo the zip, and I had to stop him. He tried to carry on, but I put my stern voice on, and spoke more loudly, and that stopped him. He hasn't tried it again."

Dawn shook her head. "Well it's time you found out how he is in bed. If he's half the man I think he is, he'll be desperate for it by now. If you don't do anything, I might try him out myself."

That really annoyed me. Grant belongs to me not her, and she shouldn't even think of that sort of thing, unless I agree to it.


~ ~ ~ ~ *Grant* ~ ~ ~ ~


We'd all had dinner together, and Harry and Dawn had drifted off, no doubt heading for a bedroom. But April had been quiet all evening.

"Listen, what's the matter? I know something's troubling you."

She frowned, and fidgeted with a table napkin. "We'll all be leaving soon, Grant."

"I know, but we've said we can meet up again when we're back home."

"Will we really though?"

I took hold of her hand. "Nothing's going to keep me away. You're in Portland and I'm in Seattle. That's less than three hours."

She smiled, and leaned across the table towards me, and we kissed.

She was still smiling. "Grant, would you like to come to my room?"

I had to restrain myself from looking too excited.

So I looked coolly at her. "That would be nice."

In her room, she poured me a drink, a large one.

"Grant, what do you think when you look at me?"

"A young woman, pretty, delicate, and cute. You know, without makeup, you could pass for a schoolgirl."

"And you'd be my teacher, no doubt."

"That would be no good. I'd be fired straight away for what I'd be thinking about doing."

She laughed. "Maybe I'll dress up as a schoolgirl sometime."

"Then maybe I'll have sex with you like that."

"Oh no you wouldn't. If you were my teacher, I wouldn't let you."

I took hold of her arms. "You couldn't stop me."

She smiled, and pulled away. "Oh yes I could, and I would."

"You're teasing me, April. I wish you'd stop that."

She came close. "I'm sorry. Will you forgive me if I let you come to bed with me?"

It was a moment before I realized what she'd said. It didn't seem real, and maybe I'd misheard, …

She giggled. "Come on, I mean it. I want you to make love to me."

In bed, naked, and with the lights out, she stroked my body, as she always did. But this time, she was exploring the part of me that she'd avoided before. In turn, I was touching her. My erection was hard, and almost becoming painful.

"April, let's make love right now."

"No, let's carry on like this. It's lovely."

I gave it a few more minutes, then I lifted myself up to a kneeling position over her.

Her legs were together, and I started pushing them apart.

She resisted, and for all her small physique, was strong enough to make it difficult.

"Grant, stop it."

"I can't stop now. I want you, and I'm going to have you."

She started struggling. "No, stop it, stop it now!"

She was getting louder. Loud enough to be heard outside the room.

I had her legs apart, but she was fighting back, like an angry cat, and I couldn't continue without hurting her. Then she shouted out loud, "Grant, stop it now."

It was too much. I gave up, and fell back onto the bed.

We'd been lying there for several minutes, not saying anything. I was seething. She'd led me along, then gone frigid on me.

She said quietly, "Grant, I told you to stop, and you didn't. If I'm to see you again, you must promise never to do that again."

The woman was a nightmare, and what pissed me off most was the thought that Harry was having it so easy with Dawn. Right then, I'd have swapped places, and let Harry try his luck here. I was trying to think how it was that I ended up with April. Just chance, I suppose.

She put her hand across to hold mine, and we lay there. As if we were two goddamn children.

It was a few minutes later that she spoke. This time, in a pleasant tone.

"You can have sex with me, but tonight is special. You'll have to do it the way I want."


Next morning, I met Harry for breakfast.

"Well, Harry, finally we had sex. And she's got experience. Definitely no virgin."

"Good then?"

"Better than good. She's a strange girl though. I was messing around, and trying it on with her, and she stopped me. So I thought that was it. But then a while later, she said it would be okay. She got out of bed, put the lights on low, and fussed around with her makeup in front of the mirror. As if that mattered. Then she came back to me. I was lying on my back, and she laid down on top of me, and started kissing. She told me what to do, and I did it. And if I varied it at all, she got annoyed, and made me keep to her script."

"Sounds intriguing. Dawn's not like that. She wants her clothes off as fast as possible."

"It was new for me. It took a hell of a long time to get to having sex, and it did all come right, but it was weird the way she acted. She directed the whole thing like a movie script, even when I was on top of her, fucking her. She talked incessantly, and in the end, I think my brain switched off."

"Sounds as if that little girl's in control of you."

"Maybe, but I've no complaints. I was ready for sex with her, so I didn't care how she wanted to do it. And she didn't disappoint. She's tiny and delicate, but she's agile too. She was all over me."

"So I guess it was worth the wait. For me, I'll always prefer quantity to quality though. They go back tomorrow, don't they?"

"Yes, late morning. We've swapped contact details, and we're definitely going to see each other again. What about you and Dawn?"

Harry smiled. "I don't think so. It turns out that there's a little matter of a husband back home."

"I suppose when I visit April, I'll see Dawn again. Maybe I'll get to meet the husband."

"He sounds ineffectual. If I were you, I'd watch out for Dawn. She's sex mad, and her husband doesn't satisfy her. You're probably on her list."

# 3

"So Grant, when you're back, you must phone or email straight away. Promise me."

"Of course I will. I've never met anyone like you, and I'm not going to let you get away."

"You'll have to come and meet my family, especially my mother."

"I hope she approves."

"Mother never approves of any man, straight away. It'll take time. And you'll have to show her respect. But you'll meet my brothers too. Ben's older than me, and Frank's younger. I think you'll get on with both of them."

"Do you see a lot of one another?"

"We're fairly close. And mother expects us all to come to the family gatherings. She's quite strict about that. You'll meet Dawn's husband too. Robin's very gentle, and soft-spoken, and a bit effeminate. Almost the opposite of you."

"So are your brothers married?"

"Frank got married young, but it broke up. And Ben's never married. He's had a few girlfriends, but it never came to anything."

"Maybe they didn't measure up to you and Dawn?"

I had to smile. Grant was nearer the truth than he realized. "You know, that might be part of it. Anyway, I have to go now."

"Goodbye kiss, then?"

"Just a brief one. Dawn's watching, and I don't want her making silly comments afterwards."

As we drove off, Dawn and I looked back, and the two men were waving.

"Look, Dawn, Grant looks so handsome. I think I will have him for my husband."

"Your prize bull?"

"You can say what you want, but he's more of a man than Robin."

She laughed. "I didn't want a prize bull. I wanted a man who would do what I want, and give me some freedom. Your Grant won't be so malleable."

"He loves me. He'll do what I want."

"But what will he let you do?"

"No one tells me what to do, but he's not the sort to even try bossing me around. Anyway, I wouldn't want to do the sort of things you have in mind."

"Maybe not now. But once you're married, you might want a little spice outside the marriage."

"I'd never put up with Grant doing that kind of thing."

"I'm talking about you, not Grant. I know you. You love attention, and having men want to touch you and kiss you. That's not going to change."

Dawn was right. But if I did anything like that, I'd be careful not to let Grant know. She doesn't care if Robin finds out, but Grant might be jealous, and annoyed too. On the other hand, it might stop him becoming complacent, and keep him attentive, knowing there's competition.

As we made our way to the airport, I daydreamed. What if Grant saw me with another man? Maybe they'd fight over me. And then the winner would take me.

# Part 2 – A BIZARRE BROTHER AND SISTER

## 4

*~ ~ ~ ~ Grant ~ ~ ~ ~*

I always hated meeting the parents of any of my girlfriends. You feel you're being inspected, with the main objective of finding faults. Still, April wasn't going to see me again, unless I met the family.

It was a regular event they have, a gathering of the family, hosted by April's mother. I was in my best clothes, and shuffled in behind April for the introductions. There were about twenty people in there, all chatting, until I came through the door. Then silence, and they all looked at me.

April announced, "Everybody, this is Grant."

She paused while they looked me over. Dawn was there, and I nodded, but she didn't respond.

"Now Grant, come and meet everyone. First, this is mother."

I smiled. "Pleased to meet you."

She looked me up and down, and then a sort of "Humph" sound, and a nod of acknowledgment, and she turned away. If she meant to be offensive, then she was doing a good job. She wasn't bad-looking for her age, but her hair up in a bun made her look like an old schoolmarm.

April moved me on. I got a more pleasant response from the others, but the only one who seemed pleased to meet me was her younger brother Frank. A big fellow, as tall as me, and well built too. But simple-minded.

The older brother Ben was almost as offhand as the mother. He was only medium height and build, but wiry, and could clearly take care of himself. He'd got a scar on his cheek, and his nose had been broken at some time. And probably not from playing sport.

It was a relief to get the introductions over with, and go somewhere quiet with April.

"I take it your mother doesn't think much of me."

"She's suspicious of new people, especially men. But you'll be all right, eventually. Don't argue with her, that's all."

"And your brother Ben wasn't much better."

"Oh, he's all right. He's very protective, and he watches out for me. When you get to know him, you'll find he's not so bad. I'm hoping you become friends."

"He looks like he can take care of himself in a fight."

"You're right there. He was terrible at school, and was even suspended a couple of times. Then after he left school he got mixed up with a bad crowd. There was one occasion where he got into a fight, with knives. Did you see the scar on his face? The young man he was fighting lost the sight in one of his eyes. It was awful seeing him in court. Ben was lucky to avoid jail. But he's calmed a lot since then."

"And your father? Where's he?"

"I suppose I should have told you. He left home when I was very young, so I barely remember him."

"And you haven't been in contact?"

"I wouldn't dream of it. Mother doesn't want us even mentioning him, so I don't think she'd take kindly to me getting in contact. Anyway, I'd have no idea where he was. Now come on, they'll be missing me."

Back in the main room, the women were all together, talking, and April walked over to join them. I was going to follow, but the circle closed, excluding me. I drifted over to where the two brothers were talking with Dawn's husband Robin. Not because I wanted to, but I couldn't stand alone in the middle of the room.

Ben looked me up and down. "Grant, a word of advice. In this family, mother's the boss. You don't butt in on her discussion. If she wants you to join in, she'll tell you."

"It's a bit limiting, isn't it?"

Frank laughed. "The last thing I'd want to do is join their chit-chat. Probably about shoes or dresses or something."

Robin said, "Frank's exaggerating, but he's got a point. I've got used to these gatherings now. You have to accept the protocol. I rely on Dawn to tell me what to do, and it keeps me out of trouble. Of course, Ben and Frank grew up with it."

Ben added, "And we like it the way it is. Now I'm ready to go off and get a drink. Robin and Grant, you'd better check you can come with us."

Robin headed to the circle of women, and I followed behind.

Dawn noticed us. "What is it?"

Robin replied, "Okay if Grant and I go for a drink with Ben?"

"Oh, all right. But don't be long."

"And Grant?"

April hadn't been facing me, but turned round now. "No, I'd rather you stayed, dear. You can make us all some coffee."

Robin started to wander off, so I said, "But I'd rather go with them."

By now a couple of them had stopped chatting, and were observing us.

Her mother said to April. "Sounds as if Grant has his own priorities. Obviously more important than ours."

I couldn't believe it. She was having a go at me, with the others watching.

April said, "I'm sorry, mother, … Grant, please come with me."

In the kitchen, she closed the door. "What's up with you? All I asked was to make some coffee. You could have looked really good doing something for them, and instead you've embarrassed me."

"I'm sorry for that, but I didn't like the way you seemed to take me for granted."

She stretched up and kissed me, with her sweet lips.

I stayed in the kitchen, and made coffee.

When I took it in, there was no "thank you" from the mother, and I was hardly acknowledged by the others, no doubt taking their cue.

As Ben and the others had gone, the only other male company was a small group of cousins, who seemed to be arguing about some longstanding family matter. The last thing I was interested in.

I went back to the kitchen, and sat down with my coffee.

What a family. The mother behaving as a female dictator. The father long gone, and who could blame him? Frank amicable enough but stupid. Then there's Ben. I'm not sure about him yet. And the cousins just a bunch of hillbillies.

Where the hell do I fit in with this crowd?


~ ~ ~ ~ *April* ~ ~ ~ ~


The get-together with my family hadn't been that successful. The introductions had gone well enough, but then Grant was so stupid. I'd asked him to be particularly careful when we were with mother, but then he had to go and argue with me, and get her annoyed. If he'd played along, we'd have got through it fine, but no, he had to be awkward. Dawn's never had any problems like that with Robin. He's a natural diplomat, and I've never seen him arguing with her.

Back at my apartment, I poured each of us a glass of wine.

"Grant, I think we need to talk."

He took a large gulp, and breathed deeply.

"That was awful. I felt second-class in there, and it's humiliating having to take that shit from your mother."

Maybe he was justified in being annoyed, but I was expecting him to apologize first. After all, he was the one most at fault.

"But the other men don't have a problem. It's maybe old-fashioned, the way she is with us all, but everyone else seems happy enough with it."

"Well, I'm different then."

He sipped his wine, and sat there, staring at his glass.

"But Grant, it's not about being different, it's about good manners, and respecting your elders."

"People have to earn respect. With me they do anyway."

I didn't know what to say. I do love him, but he can be so infuriating. He surely must realize that he has to compromise when he gets into any family.

"But you will behave when you're with them next time, won't you? Especially with mother."

"I'll try. Maybe the second time won't be so bad."

"Promise me you'll do more than try. Promise me that you'll not upset anyone."

"I can't do that. It's like I act naturally, and then you or your relatives take offense. How can I promise, when I don't know what else is going to cause the same reaction?"

He was being negative, but the drink was softening him.

"Grant, do you have to be back in Seattle any particular time?"

"No. So long as I'm at work in the morning."

"Then make me a promise, that next time you'll do everything you can to get on with my family. If you do that, then you can stay with me tonight."

# 5

No family to meet this weekend, thank goodness. I drove down from Seattle, and collected April, and we had a lovely Italian lunch, downtown in Portland.

I was in a good mood. Even gave some change to a couple of beggars. They seem younger here than any place I know. Maybe they start their begging in Portland and move south as they get older.

April and I walked in the sunshine, in the town center, and took a ride on the streetcar.

It's great being with her like this. Relaxed, and chatting about nothing in particular.

"Are you ready to head back to the car, April?"

"Yes, it's been fun. But let's get the streetcar back."

"We've three blocks to get to the stop. We might as well walk back."

"But I want to ride again. And it's quicker than walking."

"I told you it won't be quicker. By the time we get to the stop, we can be half way back to the car."

April stopped walking, and faced up to me, with her hands on her hips. "Why are you being so difficult?"

"It's simple logic. Surely you understand that?"

She swiveled on her heels, and started off back to the car park. I tagged along, gradually getting level, but only when I thought she'd cooled down.

~ ~ ~ ~ *April* ~ ~ ~ ~

Grant's been very good today, and I enjoyed being with him in town. As we walked around, I could see people looking. I'm used to men looking at me, but this was women looking at Grant too. That was almost better. I felt superior to those women, because I owned something they didn't. A nice feeling. It's the way Dawn looks at him too.

It's a pity he was so awkward with me about getting the streetcar, and I'm not sure I forgive him yet. Still, that was only one incident. Most of the time we did what I wanted.

And I needed a good day, after the problems at the office.

It was last year I got promoted to manager, and that upset a few people. They thought that because I look young and attractive, that I can't make decisions and manage people. Well, they've learned otherwise now. Naturally, I had to change the way I interacted with my colleagues, once I was their manager. They got used to that, most of them anyway.

But a couple have been difficult. So when I found that one of them had breached company rules, I wasn't unhappy about acting on it. It says quite clearly that staff are not to use the company systems for personal emails. So when I spotted a personal email on the printer out-tray, what choice did I have? The rules say that it merits a recorded verbal warning, and that's what I gave him. The others said that I should have ignored it, but the rules are clear, and there's no discretion allowed. I really had no choice.

After I'd done it, I did feel sorry for him, and I tried to get him to understand my position, but sadly he wouldn't listen, and muttered about getting a transfer. Well that would suit me fine. So a day with Grant was what I needed, to take away the stress.

But, in the evening, when he was about to leave, that earlier awkwardness was still on my mind.

"Grant, I wish you hadn't been so difficult about using the streetcar."

"But I thought I'd explained it. It was —"

"I know you'll say it's logical and all that, but it was something I wanted, and you refused. That's not very logical either, is it?"

"But we're bound to have occasional disagreements. And you can't expect me to give way every time, can you? Especially if I'm sure I'm in the right."

Grant was missing the point. If I really want something, it shouldn't be a matter of logic. If he loves me, he should be happy to go along with it. But maybe this wasn't the time to push the matter.

"I suppose you're right. But if something was important to me, you'd let me win in the end, wouldn't you?"

I pouted my lips for a kiss.

He smiled. "If it mattered that much to you, I'd do what you wanted."

# 6

I was looking forward to seeing Dawn again. She'd been offhand with me at that family gathering, making out she wasn't interested in talking to me, but I'd noticed her glancing across occasionally. Anyway that whole situation was unnatural. This had to be better, lunch in her apartment, three floors up from April's.

The only irritation was that April decided her makeup wasn't good enough, just as we were heading out, so she spent ten minutes making sure her face was perfect enough. She looks like a doll, when she wears pale makeup, with thin dark eyebrows and bright red lips. A china doll. But she's always attractive, whatever she does. And she knows it.

"Hi Dawn. Good to see you again."

Dawn welcomed me with open arms, and hugged me.

It was as if the family gathering had never happened, and we'd come straight from the vacation.

She looked to April, "Can I kiss him?"

"Of course."

But it was no kiss on the cheek. She put her hands round my neck, and stretched up to kiss me, full on my lips. April smiling, and Robin hovering in the background. That was a new one for me. But what struck me most was that she tasted of vanilla. I wondered if Harry had noticed that? Probably not. He'd have had more serious matters on his mind.

We went on through, and Robin went back to the kitchen, wearing an apron. Pink with blue flowers.

I said, "Is Robin doing the cooking?"

21

Dawn smiled. "He always does if it's something special. And I hate cooking. So what have you two been doing since that meeting with mother?"

April laughed. "Don't mention that. We've only just got over it. We've been getting on fine, haven't we, Grant?"

I nodded. "I know it's not far from Seattle, but I hadn't been to downtown Portland before, and I like it. We've had some fun there. Walking —"

Dawn shouted out, "Robin, bring some wine in here."

He came scurrying in with a couple of bottles, and then the glasses. "Sorry, Grant, I didn't think."

Dawn said, "Robin's my housewife today, aren't you darling?"

Then off he went, back to his cooking.

So this was the real Robin. A goddamn housewife.

But then I felt sorry for him. I picked up my wine. "I'll go and chat with Robin, and let you girls gossip."

In the kitchen, away from Dawn, Robin looked as self-assured as a chef.

"I'd offer to help, but I'd be no good."

"That's okay. I can manage fine. So you and April are getting along?"

"I'd say so. She's a bit overbearing, but I guess she'll mellow in time."

Robin laughed. "I doubt it. From what I've seen of her, she's much like Dawn. Used to getting their way. It's the family you know. Her mother's the boss, and they've grown up thinking that's the way it should be."

"But you don't seem to mind."

"I'm happy if Dawn's happy, and I've got used to the way she behaves. In fact, I like things the way they are."

"But hell, she called you her housewife."

"So what? What's wrong with being a housewife?"

"Nothing, I suppose. So what work do you do at the university? Some sort of professor?"

"Heavens, no. I work in the research labs. Mostly cutting up plants, and dead animals, and doing tests. Not very exciting, I'm afraid. But it brings in some money. Although not as much as Dawn."

"She sells insurance, doesn't she?"

"Yep, and she's good at it. Mostly to businesses. Come along, and I'll show you her office."

He led me to what would have been the spare bedroom. A desk in the center, with a computer, and filing cabinets along the wall.

Robin looked proud, as if it was his own. "She runs it all from here. Cold calls, then sets up meetings, and off she goes to get the sale. She used to cover Portland, but now she'll go anywhere, and do anything, to get business."

I could imagine the meeting. A purchasing officer in some large organization, with his dull little life, and then in comes Dawn. Probably suggests meeting him after work. The poor guy wouldn't stand a chance. Hell, I'd buy her insurance.

~ ~ ~ ~ *April* ~ ~ ~ ~

It was fun going to Dawn's for lunch. I had a long chat with her while Grant was in the kitchen with Robin.

"So, April, is it going to work out? It will be a while before mother takes to him, and I'm not sure he has the patience."

"I think it's going to be all right. I've told Grant what he's to do and not to do, so the next test is when we all get together again."

"Well, I do hope it works out. Let's go and see what they're up to."

In the kitchen, Robin was busy cooking, still in his apron, and Grant was lounging near him, with his wine, watching.

They didn't realize we were there to start with, then Grant caught sight of us, and jerked upright.

Dawn said, "You two look like a gay couple. Very cozy. Now Grant, don't get any ideas will you?"

23

Grant blushed, but Robin smiled.

I led Grant back to the living room, leaving Robin and Dawn.

I said, "So what do you think of Dawn's housewife. He's a good cook, isn't he?"

Grant nodded. His blush had gone now. "He's proficient all right. Probably lots of practice. But it's not very manly is it?"

"That's silly. Most of the best chefs are men, and they're manly enough."

"I know that, but he's only cooking because she tells him to."

"Well, don't worry about that kind of thing. I don't expect you to cook for us. You're not the type. Too clumsy for a start."

Grant looked thoughtful. "I wouldn't want you to be as bossy as Dawn."

"But Robin doesn't mind."

"He loves it. But I don't want you getting too much like her."

I gave him my best smile. "Surely, if I want something, and it's reasonable, then you'd want to get it for me, wouldn't you? That's not being bossy."

"It depends what you mean by reasonable."

I think I'm always reasonable, but it would be pointless explaining that one to him. He'd only twist it into an argument. As for Dawn, she's not really a domineering woman. If she wants something, Robin gets it. That's part of being married, just like sex is part of it. And when I'm married, Grant will want to do things for me too, if he really loves me.

"My darling, I promise you. When we're married, I'll make sure you never think I'm too bossy."

He smiled, and kissed me. He didn't seem to notice that I'd said "when we're married". Yet he hasn't even asked me yet. But he's the one I want. So why waste time?

# 7

The second family gathering wasn't so bad. No deathly silence when I entered, and even April's mother seemed to tolerate me. I got a thin smile at one point, which from her was more than I expected. I was on best behavior. Not that I had to do much, other than keep out of the way.

I got to talk with Ben. He's okay, but there's something strange about him. When I asked anything about the family, he'd pause a while before answering, as if deciding what he ought to tell me. Like April, he said he knew nothing about his father, but he did remember him leaving.

He works at an auto salvage yard. And that's about his only interest, apart from boxing. Frank works with him, and I thought at first that Frank did all the heavy work, but the more Ben spoke about it, it seemed that everyone there works hard. They have trouble there sometimes as well, with customers coming back complaining, thieves trying to offload stolen parts, and police looking for stolen vehicles. Ben's the guy that deals with all that shit. A tough guy in every way.

He said he could deal with anyone with his fists. So I asked what he'd do if he had to deal with two or three at the same time. From nowhere, and with a click as the mechanism triggered, he had an open switchblade knife in his hand. The narrow blade had to be six inches long, narrowing to a point. I must have looked impressed, as he smiled, and then in one smooth motion, he folded the knife and put it away.

I'd suggested staying the night at April's place, but she said it wouldn't look right, so I'd booked a hotel room downtown.

After the get-together, April came back to the hotel with me for dinner.

"Grant, you did very well today. I'm so pleased."

"It was mainly because I kept quiet and did nothing."

"It doesn't matter how you did it. These things take time, and that's the way to move things along. By the way, when we were there, I had a quiet word with mother about us getting married. I was expecting all sorts of arguments, but she was really pleased. I couldn't believe it. So you must be giving a good impression after all."

"Well, if the price to pay is keeping quiet once a month, then so be it. I can do that. So do I get a reward?"

"What sort of, ... oh, I know. Now let me think."

I leaned across and whispered, "Let's go up to my room and make love."

"If we're getting married, you'll have to save all that for the wedding night."

I must have looked so disappointed, that it made her laugh.

She said, "All right, I'll come to your room, and maybe we can play about a little. But that's all."


~ ~ ~ ~ *April* ~ ~ ~ ~


Grant had done so well at the gathering today. He hadn't upset anyone, and mother remarked how much he'd improved. Better still, she approved of him as my marriage partner. She didn't exactly say she liked him, but I could tell that she did.

After dinner at the hotel, I was in two minds about going to his room. He deserved something for his efforts, but I didn't want him going too far. We may have had sex already, but now we're engaged, it's different, and he should be willing to wait.

I told him there was to be no sex, and he agreed. But I said he could be amorous, so long as he stopped short. In bed, with the lights off, we cuddled up, chatting about the family. It was really nice, as if we were married already.

Then he started kissing me.

I expected that, and I wanted it. But when he started stroking me, he was clumsier than ever. He'd had a lot to drink with the meal, and now he was behaving like an animal, groping me. I had my panties on, and I felt him pulling at them.

"Stop it, Grant. I'm keeping them on."

But he ignored me, and kept pulling hard. Then I heard the material rip.

I tried to get up, but he held me down.

"Grant, stop it now. I've had enough."

He moved on top of me, and nearly crushed me. I tried to push him away, but it had as much effect as pushing a brick wall.

"No, Grant, we agreed no sex."

"The hell we did."

I tried to struggle, against his weight, but then I felt him push inside me, and I had to draw breath.

The alcohol had taken hold, and now I was just an object for him to have sex with, not caring if he hurt me. I tried hitting him, but he didn't even notice. So I gave up struggling, and lay there like a dead body, until he'd had enough.

After he'd got off me, I was so angry, that there were tears in my eyes. I was going to shout at him, and threaten him. But I knew that's what he'd expect, and that he probably wouldn't care, now he'd got what he wanted. So I got dressed in silence, and walked out.

He had no right to do that to me, and one way or another, he has to learn that. One day, I'll get my own back.

# 8

I'd gone too far that day. I could blame it on the drink, but that would be a lie. I was in the mood for sex, and I was in bed with her. Any man would act the same way. But now what to do? I'd tried phoning her all week, but she wouldn't reply.

I was outside her apartment building, on Saturday morning, and had hit the buzzer several times, with no answer. So I buzzed Dawn's number.

"Hi Dawn, it's Grant. Is April with you?"

"Come on up."

At her apartment, she was waiting with the door open. "Come in Grant."

I looked around. "No April then?"

"No, she's away on business. Can I get you a coffee?"

"Yes, I need one. Where's Robin?"

"Do you want to see him too?"

I felt my face flush. I wished I could stop that. It was clever, her way of putting me on my defensive.

"No, just wondering."

"You missed him. He's gone to the movie theater to see some foreign movie. Not my thing."

In the living room, I settled in the sofa. It was a nice apartment. And this room was the centerpiece. A real party room.

Dawn came in with the coffees and sat next to me. "So we're all alone, Grant, for the next couple of hours. Maybe we should get to know each other?"

I knew I could have sex with her. She had it with Harry quickly enough. And two hours be plenty. She's a good-looking woman. Not as perfect as April. But more sexy. It was tempting, but it was dangerous too. Knowing this crazy family, she might tell everything to April afterwards for the fun of it.

"All right, Dawn, tell me something about yourself."

She frowned. "There's lots of things. For example, I love big strong men like you. Now tell me what kind of women you find desirable, apart from April."

"Sexy women. Women with a nice shape."

"Do you find me sexy?"

I hesitated. "Of course I do."

She moved close and looked up at me. Her eyes closed, and we kissed. Vanilla again. Now I knew what Harry had been so enthusiastic about. She put her arms around my neck and pulled me. She was stronger than April. But I didn't mind. It was only a kiss.

Then I felt her tongue.

I pulled away. "Hey, Dawn, we shouldn't."

"I won't tell April if you won't."

"Anyway I'd better go. If April's not around, I'll head back to Seattle."

She pouted. "You can go this time. But one day I'll want more than that."

"By then, I'll be married, so I don't think so."

At the door, she came up close.

"One deep kiss, and then you can go, and I promise not to tell."

"I've trusted women before, and ended up in all sorts of trouble."

"But you can trust me. Honest, it'll be our secret. It's not as if we're having sex."

We kissed again. And this time, I let her feel my tongue too.

When we came apart, she said, "Whether you're married or not, one day I'm going to have you fuck me. That's a promise."

It's been a rough week at the office. At the mid-year review with my boss on Monday, I was told we were downsizing to save costs. I wasn't surprised, as the rumors had spread already. But what did shock me was that I had to lose two members of staff, and have them out by the end of the week.

I tried arguing for more time, but it was no use, so I had to get on with it. After all, that's what they pay me for.

I double-checked the procedures, then I interviewed them all and asked each one why they shouldn't be selected. I looked through their resumes, and their performance records.

Then I had to make my decision, and I called them all in this morning. They don't like coming in on Saturdays. But what else could I do? The procedures are laid down, and there were time delays I couldn't avoid. So if the two were to be laid off by end week, it had to be today.

In the meeting room, I went through the background to the redundancies, and then onto the criteria that have to be used. I had a woman there from Human Resources, to back me up, and be a witness that I'd done things correctly. I could tell that no one was interested, but I got through the preamble, then finally said I'd made a decision. I called out two names, a man and a woman, and asked them to come with me and the HR woman.

In my office, I had two security guards ready. Well, you never know.

The woman was sobbing. She sat down, and carried on crying into her tissues. She was no problem.

But the man didn't sit. He came and stood in front of me.

"You heartless bitch. You know about her personal problems. What's going to happen to her now?"

"I'm sorry for anyone's misfortune, but the only factors that I could take account of are those that affect the work being done. The system is fair."

"So why me?"

"Your performance reviews used to be good, but they've gone down. I'm afraid it shows a lack of commitment."

"But you did my last one. That was the worst I've had in my career, and it was totally unjustified."

"As I recall it, I'd told you on more than one occasion to do things, and you either didn't do them, or delayed doing them. The company can't tolerate that kind of attitude."

The woman had stopped crying. "Is there any appeal possible?"

"No, I'm afraid not. I've your papers here, and your final paycheck. I'll need you to hand in your access keys, and sign a declaration about company property, and that's it."

"So after five years of service, I'm to be thrown out?"

I tried to give her an understanding smile. There was no point arguing.

I went behind the desk, and sat down. "So if you both sign, then you can go."

Without warning, the man launched himself towards me across the desk, with hands outstretched. I jerked back, but the security man was faster than him anyway, thank goodness.

After the two of them had gone, I wrote some notes, and had the HR woman countersign them, in case of any arguments later. It took me nearly an hour, but it's best to be accurate and detailed regarding these things. In any case, by staying on, I could be sure no one would be hanging around outside.

Back at the apartment, I dropped in on Dawn.

"The trouble is, these people have all been issued with the company rules, and they've got detailed employment contracts, but no one ever reads them."

"Well, I never read those terms and conditions. They're so boring. By the way, Grant was here earlier."

31

I nearly dropped my coffee.

"Was he looking for me?"

"Yes. The poor guy says you won't answer his calls, so he drove down here. Haven't you punished him enough?"

"I suppose so. Maybe it's time to talk to him again. I do miss him, and after all the stress at work, I really could have done with him here. Maybe a kiss and a cuddle."

Dawn sat down next to me, on the sofa.

"As Grant's not here, I'll pretend for you."

She put her arm around me and pulled me close, and kissed me on the lips.

I had to giggle. "That's just the way Grant kisses me."

It's lovely having a sister like Dawn.

# 9

"So, Harry, will you be my best man?"

"If Dawn's going to be there, then sure thing. But how soon are we talking about?"

"April would get married tomorrow, but it's down to her mother. She wants all their family there, and make a big occasion of it. The way things are going, it'll be in about two months."

"And you're keen on the idea? I thought you enjoyed being a bachelor?"

"I'll never get anyone better than April, so why not? I'm bound to get married sometime. Start a family, and all that."

"And how's Dawn?"

"Same as ever. She had her eye on me for a while."

Harry laughed. "I told you to watch out for her. And what's her husband like?"

"Oh, Robin's okay. He's very quiet though. I don't know how they ended up married."

"Maybe he's good in bed?"

"Somehow I doubt it. But you never know."

"So have you got her an engagement ring?"

I had to laugh. "Not quite. April went and got the goddamn thing herself. Of course I got the bill. Way into four figures."

"So you didn't go down on your knees to propose, if she'd already got the ring?"

"I didn't propose at all. We just reached a point where we knew we'd be getting married."

"What about her mother? You know what they say about girls becoming like their mothers."

33

"I hope not. She can be a bitch. When you're at the wedding, you're best to keep clear of her. And April's brothers are no great fun either. Frank's the younger one, and he's stupid, and Ben's strange. Sometimes he's okay, then other times I see him watching me. A cold look, like he resents me being with April. Probably thinks I'm not good enough."

Harry smiled. "This wedding's going to be fun then."

"You'll meet the brothers at my bachelor party. Maybe you'll get on better than I have."

"Well, if this Ben gives me the cold stare, I might punch him one."

"Don't even think about it. He's a born fighter."

Best not to tell Harry about the knife.

~ ~ ~ ~ *April* ~ ~ ~ ~

Everything's coming together now.

Mother's made all the arrangements, and Dawn's to be my bridesmaid.

It's hard to believe that it's not long since I first met Grant, yet here we are.

I love my engagement ring, and can't keep from looking at it. Grant was awkward about my buying it, but I'm the one that's to wear it, so why shouldn't I choose it?

Grant is like that sometimes, but once we're married, and he's living with me, I'm sure he'll settle down and behave more sensibly. And if he is awkward about changing his ways, I'll do what I have to. He's so desperate to please me, that I wouldn't have to do much. Maybe give him stony silences. I'm good at that. And if all else fails, I can deprive him of other pleasures for a while.

Dawn's been quite excited about the wedding. She's never been a bridesmaid before, and she's keen to help with everything. However, we did have a little argument over her dress. It's surely for me to decide what the bridesmaid wears, but she didn't approve of my choice, and wanted something much too revealing. I told her that I should be the center of attention, and not her. But in the end, we compromised, as we usually do when we argue over something.

She's aware that Harry will be coming, and I'm sure she's got something planned. Poor Robin will be left on his own. Maybe he'll flirt with one of the waitresses, or even one of the waiters.

Ben's been a bit of a nuisance. He's been coming to my apartment, and hanging around to chat. He is useful at times, but he was getting on my nerves, so I had to tell him to stop coming unless he was invited. He ought to get a steady girlfriend or even get married. That would keep him occupied.

He doesn't want me marrying Grant. I don't know if his problem is with Grant, or with the fact that I'm getting married. Either way, I don't care. He even said that if Grant gives me trouble, he'll come and deal with it. I told him I can manage perfectly well without his help, but he is so insistent. It's as if he wants me to have a problem I can't deal with.

And that's probably because he wants another reward from me. Well, I'm getting tired of him and his rewards. Once I'm married, I won't need him to do things for me, and he can go his own way.

# 10

My bachelor party was a quiet affair. Robin, and the brothers Ben and Frank. Then Harry and three work colleagues down from Seattle.

Harry topped up his beer from the pitcher, then raised his glass. "A toast, everyone, to Grant. His last days of freedom."

I smiled, as they raised glasses too, and drank to me.

The last half-hour, we'd been watching the end of a game on the big screen, and drinking beer, so not much said. But it was relaxed, and maybe a good way to get to know Ben and Frank better. Hell, they'd be family before long.

Harry said, "So what's the job you're moving to? Same sort of thing?"

"It's power supply equipment, not aircraft components. But testing is much the same anywhere. Read the plans, do the tests, and write up the results."

"Was it difficult getting the job?"

"Not at all. The company's got some new contracts and they're recruiting like crazy. So I interviewed, and then got the offer on the spot. And it pays well too, although not as much as my job in Seattle."

"You didn't think of you two moving to Seattle then?"

"I'm not sure we even talked about it. Probably harder for her to get a job quickly there."

Ben said, "And she wouldn't want to be that far from her family."

Harry laughed. "It's only three hours for God's sake. We've just driven down here."

Ben muttered, "Nevertheless."

Time to change the subject. "Frank, are you looking forward to the wedding?"

Frank leaned forward beaming. "I sure am. I'll be at the church door, handing out the books. I've already tried my suit on. I'm going to be real smart."

One of my friends looked across, grinning and rolled his eyes.

But Ben saw it. His face flushed, and he leaned forward aggressively. "What's that expression about?"

"I wasn't looking towards you, I was looking at Grant. It was a private joke."

Ben stood up. "At my brother's expense?"

His stance was hostile, and his face muscles taut, like a boxer out of his corner.

The reply came in a weaker voice, "No, I wasn't meaning to get at anyone. I'm sorry, Ben, I didn't mean anything."

Ben sat back down, still tensed. Robin looked cowed, even though it was nothing to do with him. And Frank didn't even know what was going on.

After that, the relaxed atmosphere never returned. We talked a little, but found it convenient to watch the big screen, even though it was only some women's soccer.

Finally, Harry took the inevitable glance at his watch, and gave the "must be going" excuse. And so the event was over.

Across town, April was having her own party. It had to be better than this one.

I headed back to the hotel with Robin. Dawn didn't want him back before midnight.


~ ~ ~ ~ *April* ~ ~ ~ ~


Dawn had organized my party. It was a new bar downtown, and we'd dressed up. Dawn and me, and three friends. Dawn had arranged for a limo to take us there, so that we could all drink. We had champagne to start with, then Dawn announced we were moving on, so we had a round of tequila shots.

And off we went, back in the limo.

Dawn wouldn't say where we were going, but when we got there I knew straight away. I'd heard of it, but never thought I'd go there. A club for gays. Men and women, but all gay. We were all giggling by now, as we went in, and found a table.

I said, "Why on earth have you brought us here, Dawn?"

"I wanted to see what it was like. It seemed a bit of fun. Anyway we won't be here long. I've got something much more special planned."

So more champagne, until I was almost dizzy.

At one point, a woman came along and asked me to dance, and I politely refused. Then afterwards, Dawn and the others kept on at me that I was chicken, and should have gone with her. She was nice looking, but I'd have felt silly. And who'd be leading, anyway? A bit embarrassing, but I was pleased it was only me that anyone wanted to approach. I think Dawn would have gone with her, and was envious, and that made me even more satisfied. Maybe that's why I was still thinking about it, long afterwards.

Then off we went again, and before long, we were in Dawn's apartment.

I had to stop drinking, as I was feeling dizzy again, but the others had more champagne. It was a great girls' night. Chatting about men and relationships, and lots of comments and advice about what lay ahead for me. They'd all love to sleep with Grant, I'm sure of it.

I thought that was it for the evening. Then the doorbell rang. Dawn brought him into the room. A hulk of a man, as big as Grant. And very handsome. Carrying a case.

Dawn said, "This is our entertainment for the evening. Say 'hello' everyone."

Then she pointed him to the bedroom, and came back. "He's a stripper. Let's rearrange the furniture."

By the time he came in, in a tuxedo, we were all sitting in a row, along two sofas, with me in the middle, and Dawn next to me.

He'd got a music player with him, and started it up. Sensual music. I decided it was time to have my glass of champagne.

Then he got going. Moving rhythmically to the music, taking off his clothes one by one, with us girls quiet to start with, then getting noisier, as it progressed. When his shirt came off, his chest was gleaming. He'd oiled the skin, and it looked beautiful. Then his pants, and showed off his legs. Shaved and oiled. Dawn was shouting by now for him to take his thong off. But he was clever at what he did. No rush, but moving towards us provocatively at times, and swaying to the music.

Dawn said, "He's got a perfect body, like Grant's."

I smiled. "Grant's more muscular, but this guy's so sexy with his skin all shiny."

"Maybe you'll have to get Grant to do the same then? I'll put the oil on if you don't want to get messy."

Finally, the man took off his thong. His penis was enormous, and he let it sway to the music. Then he came close, and stood in front of me.

He said, "Why don't you touch it?"

"No, I'm not doing that."

He didn't move, but looked to the others. They started telling me to do it, and then they were all getting louder and shouting in unison.

I put my hand out and touched it —

He jumped away, and laughed, and then carried on dancing until the music stopped. Finally he took a bow, and we all applauded.

After he'd left, Dawn got us coffee, and we sobered up a little.

One of the girls asked, "Did it feel funny, touching him?"

"Not really. It was like touching dead meat."

"Not the same as touching Grant's then."

"I'm not saying. But if that had been Grant stripped off, it wouldn't be hanging loose."

The girl said, "Maybe this guy's gay?"

Dawn laughed. "Then maybe I should have let Robin stay with us."

We all giggled at that.

Then Dawn said, "Anyway, we don't need to hire a stripper next time. April says we can have Grant do a show for us."

I put down my coffee. "I said no such thing."

"He'd be good at it though, wouldn't he? Admit it."

"I suppose so, …"

# Part 3 – WEDDING AND HONEYMOON AFFAIRS

## 11

~ ~ ~ ~ *Grant* ~ ~ ~ ~

The wedding was a blur.

April's mother had it organized like a military operation, and I had instructions every step of the way. I suppose it's the woman's day, so maybe that's always how things are at weddings.

April has a lot of relatives, nearly all living in Oregon. Two aunts and an uncle, and lots of cousins. Even dressed up, the men still looked like hillbillies, and I'd guess there's some inbreeding going on. But the women looked okay.

Not many on my side had bothered to make the journey down to Oregon. As my parents are long gone, the family hasn't really kept in contact. One of my uncles, a cousin, and a couple of college friends, as well as Harry and some recent friends and colleagues.

Dawn looked stunning as the bridesmaid. If April didn't look so good herself, I'd have been thinking I was marrying the wrong one. Harry was almost salivating.

So I followed my script. Said yes. Swapped wedding rings, the ones April had paid for this time. Kissed the bride. Then off to the reception for lunch, and the speeches. Mine as boring as any, but I kept it short.

The best part was the dancing afterwards. April and I took to the floor first, for a formal dance, then it was open house. April drifted off, dancing mainly with her cousins, and I picked out some nice girls as my partners. Then Dawn got hold of me. She dances close, real close, and I could feel every shape of her body against mine. For a while, she went off with Harry somewhere, but she was back before long, and dancing with me again. Then April came out of nowhere. So after that it was just me and April. Nice to have two women after me.

~ ~ ~ ~ *April* ~ ~ ~ ~

The wedding was perfect. Everyone did what they should, and there were thankfully no mistakes. Grant behaved beautifully too, and I was proud of him. When we had the practice session last week, he'd messed up his lines, and I'd been quite angry with him. But today he was word-perfect.

Dawn was irritating though. She was flirting with the men, before and after the ceremony. I wouldn't mind if she kept to Harry, but she was all over the place, and was a distraction I could have done without. Robin either doesn't notice or doesn't care.

But having said that, she was the perfect bridesmaid. It's at times like this that I would have wanted my father to be around. I've been told he wasn't interested in his children, but I'm sure he would have been proud of me today, and would have led me up the aisle. My uncle did it okay, but it's not the same. It made me wonder where my father might be right now, whether he was even alive, maybe still living in Oregon, and not far away.

The reception was fun. After the speeches, I had my dance with Grant, and then we swapped around a little. I was happy enough until I saw him with Dawn once too often, so I butted in, and hung onto him after that. For goodness sake, she had Robin there, and Harry. But what was most irritating was that Grant seemed to be encouraging her. Anyway, before long the limo came to take us to the airport. We were on our way. To our honeymoon and a married life.

# 12

It was late when we got to the hotel.

The room was great, with fantastic views, so we got room service. It was a pretty good end to the day, looking out over the moonlit beach, sipping a whiskey sour. The wedding seemed so long ago after the traveling, and I was tired. But this was our wedding night, so I took a shower, and I was ready enough then. Hell, I'd been waiting long enough for it.

But it wasn't my choice. When we were in bed, April said she was tired too, so "let's just relax together tonight". Within minutes, she was asleep, and I was lying there, wide awake, regretting that I'd freshened up.

Next morning, after breakfast, we went for a walk. It's a beautiful place, and we walked miles before we got back for lunch. Then we settled by the pool.

It wasn't long before April drew attention. Some young men and women were playing volleyball in the court nearby, and one of the women came over. They were a woman short, and would April like to play? I nodded okay, and said I'd be in the bar. I watched for a few minutes. She was good, and outclassed a couple of them.

I headed for the bar, and got myself a cold beer. That's when she turned up. Probably early fifties, and with a husky voice from too many cigarettes, but very sexy.

She was carrying an ice bucket, and said to the barman, "Fill it up again, will you. That damned machine's still not working."

Then she noticed me. "I can't stand not having ice, and I reported it this morning. It's a real nuisance carrying this upstairs each time, and I wait forever for room service."

It was instinctive I suppose. Damsel in distress. Well, not exactly a damsel.

"Let me bring it up for you. I'm at a loose end."

I'd hardly got in the door when she was on me, kissing and with her hands wandering where they shouldn't. But I was bottled up from yesterday, especially that dance with Dawn. So why not? April's having her fun. Why shouldn't I have mine? That's how I ended up in bed with her.

So my wedding night, somewhat delayed, was with this woman. And it was one hell of a wedding night. She had so much energy, and wanted to use it all up on me.

Then, when she started slowing, I took charge, and gave her as good as she gave me.

The funny thing was, I don't think either of us said more than a few words all the time I was in there, until I said I'd have to go. Silent sex. Well, not totally silent.

~ ~ ~ ~ *April* ~ ~ ~ ~

It's lovely here by the beach. Grant and I have walked around, and everywhere is pretty. I'm so glad I chose this place, in spite of the travel. I thought Grant would be annoyed about not having sex on our wedding night, but he was very understanding, so I'll have to make a special effort from now on.

After lunch, some young folks invited me to play volleyball. I've played before, and I think I surprised them with how good I was, considering I'm not very tall.

Then they all wanted to take a walk, but I said Grant would be waiting. I checked the bar, but he'd gone. Probably resting in the room. I thought of going up there, but I knew it would be more fun on the beach, so I ran and caught up with the others.

One of the boys was unattached, and he homed in on me. When he held his hand towards mine, I took hold, and we walked along as if we were teenagers on a date. After a while, the others were getting further away from us.

44

I said, "Should we catch up?"

He smiled. "No, let's sit a while."

It suited me. I'd walked enough in the morning. We sat under the shade of a tree, by the beach, and chatted a while. Then the inevitable.

"You're very beautiful, April. I wish you didn't have a boyfriend already."

I giggled. "Actually, he's not really a boyfriend."

He leaned towards me. He was so young, maybe not even twenty. I closed my eyes, and let him kiss me. It was so nice lying there with him, exchanging kisses like young lovers. I'm married to Grant, and I'll never leave him. But what he doesn't know won't hurt him. And this was so delicious.

He seemed happy to be kissing, and didn't try anything else. Maybe that was just as well, in case Grant came along. When we both sat back again, holding hands, I said, "Which room are you in?"

He answered, and then, "Why do you want to know?"

"Oh, I'm interested in all sorts of things. And you're sharing?"

"With my friend, yes." Then a pause. "But I can have the room to myself if I want it."

It was fun flirting with him. I don't think I'll do anything more with him, and be content with this little scene on the beach. But now, his imagination's probably out of control. The poor boy.

I got up. "It's been lovely, but I must go."

When I got back, Grant was by the pool. I was nervous, as I'd been away well over an hour.

But he looked up, smiling. "Hi honey, everything okay?"

"Yes, fine. After the game, you weren't here, so I walked down the beach with them. They're a lot of fun. But have you been sitting here bored?"

"No, I've been fine."

I leaned down and kissed him. "You're a perfect husband."

We got to bed at a decent time tonight, and we made love. It was a perfect wedding night, although Grant didn't seem as desperate as I'd have expected, after waiting so long.

Afterwards, lying there, I was thinking of my nineteen-year-old boy. He's probably a virgin, and would be scared stiff if I did go to his room. Grant's what I want for a husband though. Not some weedy teenager.

But that doesn't mean I can't flirt with him. Dawn does it all the time, so why shouldn't I? She even flirts with Grant, and he lets her do it. Maybe even encourages her.

So maybe I'll see my teenager again tomorrow.

# 13

~ ~ ~ ~ *Grant* ~ ~ ~ ~

It's been a great week. Apart from the first night, sex every night with April.

She seems to enjoy being with those teenagers. It's obvious that one boy's got a crush on her, the way he looks at her, and the sly way he checks me out. It's good for her ego, and maybe that's why she's so ready for sex at night.

They play volleyball each afternoon, then go off for a walk. She's so dainty, she looks like a teenager herself when she's with them. Maybe I should feel jealous that she's off with them so much, but it suits me fine, as I can stretch out by the pool, and work out in the hotel gym. And get in shape for the evening.

I saw that older woman again, one evening in the restaurant. She was with some guy who must have been in his seventies. Someone ought to warn him. She could give him a heart attack the way she performs. I did wonder about going another round with her, but frankly, I'm getting enough of it from April.

Today I'm off fishing. A couple of guys here have rented a boat, so we're heading off with a few cases of beer. April seemed put out, but it's only one day, and it's an opportunity not to be missed.

~ ~ ~ ~ *April* ~ ~ ~ ~

This honeymoon has been everything I dreamed it would be, and more. Grant's been so wonderful, and we've had time together to walk and visit things. And he's been so good about my joining in with those young people.

47

That boy's been persistent, and getting more daring through the week. He's probably told his friends, and then he's been encouraged to try more. He tried groping me a couple of times, but I stopped him. Not in an angry way, but taking his hand and moving it back.

But this morning I was annoyed with Grant. He'd decided to go on a fishing trip for most of the day. And it was clear that women weren't welcome. So I was at a loose end.

When we were walking down the beach in the afternoon, I said to my boy, "Would your room be free right now?"

He went red, and nearly tripped over in the sand. "Just a minute."

He ran forward to his friend, and pulled him aside, then came back to me. "Yes, it's free as long as I want it."

"Then let's go back. I'm so hot, I need to cool off."

As we got near to the hotel, he let go of my hand. Panicky I suppose. I said, "Hold my hand, please. Grant's not around."

By now he knew that I was married, and he was nervous of Grant. Which added to the fun of it.

His room was a mess. Two young men not caring what the place looked like. Not that I cared either. At least the maid had changed the bedclothes.

I only had my bikini on, and he had his shorts.

I lay down on my back, and beckoned to him. "Come and kiss me."

He didn't hesitate, but threw himself on me, and started kissing, and fondling. This time I didn't stop him. He got more and more excited, until finally I pushed him off. "Have you got a condom?"

He stuttered, "Yes."

"Then for heaven's sake put it on."

While he was taking his shorts off, and slipping it on, I took off my bikini, and lay back down on the bed. I spread my hair out on the pillow, thinking that would look nice, especially if it was his first time.

He was on me again like a rabbit, and immediately pushed his little tool into me and started humping. Like Grant, he had no finesse.

But it was different from sex with Grant, having a man on top who's hardly bigger than me. All I could think was that Grant was off killing fish, and here I was underneath my lively little teenager. Fair exchange.

He'd soon finished, and then was exhausted, so I pushed him over to lie next to me.

He said quietly, "Was that all right?"

The boy wanted reassurance. And why not? "It was perfect. You're quite a man in bed."

I knew he was smiling without even looking. He would be telling all his college friends soon. But what now? Grant wouldn't be back for a while yet. We'd been lying there about a quarter-hour, and we'd both cooled off.

I said, "Let's have a shower."

"What, together?"

"Any objections?"

The shower was what I needed. A wet room, with heaps of warm water raining down. And I had company.

I said, "Wash me, will you? You can start at my neck and work downwards."

I closed my eyes, and his delicate hands smoothed soap on me, and worked it round and down my body. He took a long time washing my breasts, and then even longer lower down. It was luxurious, better than any spa treatment.

I said, "Stop now, and kiss me."

He stood and came up against me, and kissed me nervously.

I said, "Now close your eyes, and I'll give you a little reward."

I knelt down, to face his penis. It was hard, and the water from the shower was dripping off it.

I put my mouth around it, and heard him whimper.

Then I sucked it gently, and ran my fingertips over his testicles. He was making little noises now, like a girl having her first sex.

49

It wasn't as big as Grant's, and I could get it all inside my mouth, and feel it with my tongue. Then I gently closed my teeth on it.

I could feel his body pulsing, so it was getting near. But I timed it perfectly. I'd got off him, and out of the way, just when he ejaculated. I stood up behind him, and pulled his back towards me, holding him tight as his body shook, with the water streaming over us.

He'd be smiling, and so happy. I was smiling too. I'd never done that before.

I love being married. But it's fun having boyfriends too.

# 14

~ ~ ~ ~ *April* ~ ~ ~ ~

"I tell you, Dawn, that was the best vacation I've ever had. I'm going to enjoy married life, I know it."

"But it's not a honeymoon every day, you know. And did Grant have a good time too?"

"He loved it. We had the mornings together, then he spent his afternoons by the pool and in the gym, while I went to the beach, and then we'd have the evenings together."

"And I take it you consummated the marriage?"

"We were both too tired the first night, but every night after that was fine."

"So what were you doing while he was in the gym?"

"Oh, I met up with some young people, and hung out with them in the afternoons. They were a girl short for volleyball, so it worked out fine. Then we'd go for walks along the beach."

"Sounds almost romantic. You should have had Grant along."

I hesitated. But I always tell Dawn eventually. "Actually, there was a boy there that was unattached, so I tended to walk with him."

"Oh yes? And what else."

"Nothing really. Walking and sometimes sitting and talking."

"Tell the truth, April. I always know if you're not. What else?"

"Well, he did kiss me a few times. But that's all."

"Now I know you're lying. I can see it in your eyes. So how often?"

"How often what?"

"You know what I mean. How many times did you have sex with him?"

"I didn't have … Well, we did have sex one time, but that's all."

Dawn smiled. "No wonder you had a nice honeymoon. But if Grant ever found out what you got up to, there'd be fireworks. Women on honeymoon don't usually have sex with other men."

"I know that, but there's no harm done. I love Grant just the same. Maybe I even appreciate him more now."

Dawn laughed. "I'm sure he'd be pleased to hear that. So why don't you tell him?"

"I might, one day. I'll have to think about it."

"And what if he told you that he was doing something like that too? Maybe someone he met at the gym, while you were having your walk?"

"If he was, then he's clever at hiding it."

"But you wouldn't mind if he did?"

"Of course I would. I should be enough for him."

"It works both ways, at least that's the way he'd see it."

"Well, that's not the way you and Robin are. Robin knows what you get up to, and he doesn't do anything himself."

"Yes, but I don't actually tell Robin anything. He might guess, but that's not the same as telling him. If you want my advice, do the same with Grant, and keep quiet about your beach boy."

~ ~ ~ ~ *Grant* ~ ~ ~ ~

We've been back at April's apartment a couple of days now, and I've started at my new job. It's a good lot of people there, helpful too, and the work's similar to what I'd done before. So give it a week or two, and I'll be up to speed. The only downside is that my new boss is a woman, and so it's like I've got women directing me 24/7.

When I told April, she got tense, especially when I told her Tiffany is divorced. But when I said that she was plain and seriously overweight, it calmed her down. Actually, Tiffany would do well to lose a couple of pounds, but she's anything but plain.

April got me into a strange conversation last night, lying in bed.

"Grant, we've got to be faithful to each other. But what does that mean exactly?"

I probably flushed thinking of the right answer, so it was handy that the lights were out. "I suppose basically, I don't have sex with other women, and you don't have sex with other men."

"But what about say, kissing?"

"I'd say that's ruled out too, if you mean on the lips."

"Sometimes you can end up in a situation where it's difficult to avoid that kind of thing. Don't you agree?"

My stomach tensed. Maybe she saw me with that woman at the hotel bar. "That's true. Neither of us should go out looking for anything, but situations do arise."

"And that wouldn't be unfaithful, would it?"

Then silence.

I thought we'd finished. Then a few minutes later she said, "That boy tried it on with me, you know. It wasn't my fault."

So she didn't know about me. It was something she'd done. I relaxed.

"What did he do?"

"On that last day, when you were away fishing, he took advantage of me. I told him off, and said I'd report him. And I would have done, but he looked so frightened, that I decided that was punishment enough."

"So what did he do, kiss you, or more than that?"

"Yes he kissed me, but I don't want to get into detail. It'll make me remember it."

We lay there in silence. It pissed me off that something had gone on there, and she wasn't telling me. For all I knew, the little creep had screwed her.

She came closer to me, and whispered, "Do you forgive me?"

"I suppose so."

She cuddled up close.

I said, "Would you forgive me if I said I'd done something like that?"

"No I wouldn't."

"But fair's fair."

"It's not the same. If it happens to a woman, it's because a man starts it. But if it happens to a man, it's almost certain the man wants it. But you haven't done anything, have you?"

"No. I was only asking."

# 15

This week, I had to do the annual appraisals for my staff, and that always causes a certain amount of tension. The guidelines say that on average a manager should rate only ten per cent of her people as outstanding, and another twenty percent as excellent. And that's exactly what I did. But as happened last year, some of them grumbled about being rated only as satisfactory. I can't blame them, as it does affect their salary increases and their promotion prospects. But I can't say they're all excellent, as it tells my boss that I can't rate people. Anyway, most of them are anything but excellent.

The annoying thing is that some other managers are exceeding the percentages, and getting away with it, and that gets my people even more irritable. But my record looks good to my own boss.

He's in his fifties, and looks quite distinguished. Over the desk from me, he took off his glasses, looked at me, and frowned. He said he intended to rate me as excellent or outstanding, but hadn't decided which. Then he had a meeting to go to. That's why he offered to discuss my appraisal at the end of the day. He was so transparent.

It was nearly six before he called me up to his office. Everyone on his floor had already left, so it was eerie. When I got to his office, I could tell what was on his mind. He has a nice little area with a sofa and coffee table, and he was sitting there, not at his desk.

"Come and sit down, April. Glass of wine?"

I thought, why not? He's even got a minibar in here.

"So how are you getting on as a manager? Enjoying it?"

"I love it. And do you think I'm doing a good job? Compared to other managers?"

"You're all doing well, but I'd rank you in the top few."

He shuffled slightly closer, pretending he was getting comfortable. He was itching to make contact.

I looked up at him, wide-eyed. "It's only because I'm working for you. Whatever the hassle I get, I feel protected, and that you think of me as someone special. Is that being silly?"

He smiled, but hesitantly. He was cautious, gradually moving closer, and his face getting nearer. Very cautious. Probably worried about being accused of harassment. I closed my eyes.

Then he kissed me, and he was mine.

So it was kissing and embracing for maybe ten minutes, and then he was ready for the next stage, undoing a button on my blouse. Time to pause.

I pulled away. "No we mustn't."

"Are you upset with me?"

"No. It's just, … well, not tonight."

He smiled, and topped up the glasses.

"I've decided to rate you as outstanding."

I couldn't help squeal with delight, and I gave him a quick kiss on the cheek. "Oh, thank you. That's wonderful."

His smile was even broader. "I suppose we both need to be getting home. Is there anything else I can do for you, April?"

I hadn't expected that, and I had to think quickly. "Not really, but now you mention it, you know that little group that deals with claims? I've always thought it would make more sense if it came under me."

He frowned. "That's Scott and two or three others? Yes, it probably does make sense. Thanks for the suggestion. I'll think about it."

I knew he'd do more than think. It will be lovely to have Scott working for me.

Grant was annoyed with my being late. I've told him I need to work after hours sometimes, and he accepts that, but then he argued that I should have phoned. I said it was difficult, and he said surely it's not, and on we went. Sometimes I feel I can't win with him.

Anyway, he shouldn't need to know where I am, every minute of the day. In fact, I don't want him to know. It would be as if I was being spied on all the time. I cut the argument short by telling him of my rating. He's very supportive, and there's no question he was pleased. So although I was annoyed about the argument, I decided to forgive him.

~ ~ ~ ~ *Grant* ~ ~ ~ ~

April is inconsiderate at times. This evening, she was late back from work without any apology. What got me was that she'd not bothered phoning, and I'd started to wonder whether something had happened to her. And she's told me not to phone her at the office, unless it's an emergency.

So the usual argument, but for once I got the better of her, as I was clearly in the right about the phone call. I'm pleased she's doing well there, with her appraisal and all that, but she shouldn't be letting it interfere with her home life. I told her that, but then she brought up that she was earning more than me, and that if she was to build a career, it was inevitable that there'd be some effect at home. So she won that one.

We didn't speak much after that until later on in the evening, after we'd eaten.

She suddenly exclaimed, "Oh my nail! The varnish has chipped away."

I looked and could hardly see a problem. She could have touched it up, but instead of that, she removed it from all her fingers and put on new varnish.

So we were sitting there, watching TV, with her hands held out to dry, and the smell of varnish pervasive.

She said, "My feet are so hot."

"What do you want me to do about it?"

"Darling, would you get a bowl, and wash my feet for me? I can't do anything with my nails drying."

"Hell, April, can't you wash them yourself when your nails are dry?"

"That'll be ages. And it's not that much to ask. Robin washes Dawn's feet for her, and he doesn't grumble."

"Well, I'm not Robin."

We sat in silence watching the TV. If I didn't wash her goddamn feet, she was going to be in a mood for the rest of the evening, and when we went to bed. "All right, I'll get a bowl."

"And use the lavender soap, darling, and bring some talcum powder."

So a strange scene. There I was, washing her feet, then carefully drying them, and all the while, she was watching the TV, laughing at what was on, seemingly oblivious of me.

She's such tiny feet, like a little doll. When I'd dried them, I stroked them a little, to feel the soft skin. Then I rubbed them over with the talc. And still no reaction from April. I tidied up and took the things away, then sat back down myself.

When the program finished, she looked down at her feet and flexed them. "That's lovely, Grant. I might let you do that again."

# 16

It was a few days later, when I got the phone call that caused all the trouble.

Already eight in the evening, and April was still not back. I tried phoning her, and it went to voicemail. So I was stressed enough before the phone rang. But it was her mother.

"Tell April I want to speak to her."

It wasn't the words, but the superior tone with which she said it. I'd had enough of this shit.

"What did you say?"

"I want to speak to April."

That did it. "Do you ever say 'please'?"

There was a pause, and I could feel the tension.

Finally she blurted out, "How dare you. She's my daughter —"

I slammed the phone down.

It was about an hour later that the door entry buzzed. It was April's two brothers. On the intercom, Ben said, "We need to talk."

I let them in, and took them through into the living room. They'd looked amiable enough, but then, without warning, Frank grabbed me from behind, holding me tight. I'm stronger than most, but he's big, and had the advantage. I couldn't move.

Ben came to stand in front of me.

"Grant, if you ever talk to my mother like that again, I'll make your life a misery."

"She was rude to me. No one treats me —"

He punched me in the stomach. He was so fast, I didn't even have time to brace myself.

It made me gasp for breath. I couldn't work out how he could do that without a big swing. I'd have doubled up, but for Frank holding me tight.

Ben said, "That's a taste. And in future, if my mother wants something, you do it. No questions, no smart remarks, and no fucking around. Do you understand?"

What choice did I have? "I understand. I'll do what she says."

"Well, let's be sure you remember."

He punched me again in the stomach. This time I was ready, and tensed my muscles to take the blow. It helped, but as I went forward, with the pain, he brought his fist up into my face. Frank let go of me and I fell to the floor.

After they'd gone, I had to lie there for a while, to let the pain subside. Then I went to the bedroom to see what I looked like.

My stomach was pink from the impact, but my face was worse. Where he'd hit me, the cheek was red, and my eye was half-closed with the swelling. I was going to have one hell of a black eye.

I showered and got dressed, and waited for April. So this was married life. Sitting here on my own waiting for her. And that damned family in the background.


~ ~ ~ ~ *April* ~ ~ ~ ~


When I got home, at about eleven, I knew something was up.

I'd had dinner with my boss, at a lovely Italian restaurant, and I didn't regret it, whatever mood Grant was in. I was expecting him to be unpleasant about my being late, so I was ready for that, and for his questions, and I had a good story ready. However, I seemed to be the least of his problems.

He was sitting in the living room, reading the newspaper, and I thought he was sulking, until he turned towards me. His face looked terrible, a dark bruise down one side, and his eye closed and swollen.

I rushed to him. "Oh, Grant, what's happened to you?"

He looked grim. "It was your brothers. They came round here, and Ben punched me, while Frank held me. It's Ben that's responsible. Frank was doing what he was told."

"But why?"

"It was your mother started it. She phoned up, asking for you, and I guess I was a bit abrupt. Then next thing I know, Ben's round here saying I've offended her, and that was his justification."

"Well, you shouldn't have upset her, but Ben's no right to come here and do that."

Ben does infuriate me sometimes, the way he always wants to interfere. If he had an issue with Grant, he should have discussed it with me first.

I picked up the phone, and dialed. "Ben, I'm coming round."

He was looking sheepish when I arrived, and rightly so.

He said, "It's about Grant isn't it?"

"Yes. You've made a terrible mess of his face. What on earth caused all the trouble?"

"He started it. Mother had phoned to talk to you, and Grant was offensive with her."

"What did he say?"

"I don't know, but whatever it was, she was fuming. I think she had to phone someone to talk to, and I was it. So I got Frank, and went round to your place. And you know the rest."

"I don't know what to say. Grant shouldn't have upset her like that, but you really hurt him."

"So should we let him treat her any way he wants?"

"No, of course not. But did you have to be so violent? His eye's in a terrible state."

"If you'd been there, it might have been different, but when I saw him, he seemed so arrogant. And then thinking of mother, I overreacted. So will you forgive me?"

"I don't know. I still think you were too harsh."

He came close to me. "If you ever have a problem with Grant, let me know. I'm not going to let him insult mother, but he ought to know that the same goes if he upsets you too."

Ben was looking at me so eagerly. Looking for forgiveness. And maybe I would want his help some time. There were tears forming in his eyes.

Being married's a good thing, and Grant's the best husband I can imagine. But he does need to be kept in check.

I gave Ben a kiss, on the lips. He always likes that.

"I forgive you, Ben."

# 17

April's working late again, and it's getting towards eleven o'clock, so I might as well go to bed. When she gets in, she likes me to be up, but she'll want to unload about the office politics.

Staying late there might be good for her career, but if I'm being left on my own too often, that's not good for the marriage. And there could be more to it. I wouldn't put it past her to be having an affair with someone there, but there's no way of knowing.

I had to smile, thinking of my own boss, Tiffany. Maybe I should offer to work late with her sometime. Then I wonder how April would feel?

It's three months now since the wedding, and it's settling into a pattern. She's not the sweet and innocent thing that I thought she was when we first met, but I was becoming aware of that by the time we married, so I can't complain.

The big complication is the family. Her brothers are suitable cases for a psychiatrist, and her cousins are pretty well all inbred.

April, Dawn and their mother seem to be the exceptions in this weird crowd.

But Dawn's becoming an irritation. It was flattering enough to start with, with her attentions, and I know sex would be good. But those two are too close. Dawn would probably tell April next day, and then I'd have another problem to deal with. Not that she could criticize, after letting that boy chase after her on the honeymoon.

Their mother's a puzzle. Her attitude to me has been confusing. Sometimes she seems to approve of me, and at other times she's offhand, as if I'm not good enough for them. But I don't think that's her real character. Maybe trying to keep this family organized is what's shaping her behavior. I'd hate to have the job myself.

So am I happily married? Hard to say. When I weigh it all up, married life isn't what I expected, but it's still pretty good. And I wouldn't want to be married to anyone but April.

Maybe I'll stay up a bit longer.

# Part 4 – FIRST LESSON IN DOMINATION

# 18

~ ~ ~ ~ *Grant* ~ ~ ~ ~

I knew April was lying.

"You must think I'm a fool. No one works that late. Has someone been fucking you?"

"No they haven't. Why do you always think the worst of me, Grant?"

"Because it's one o'clock in the morning, and I know what you can get up to."

"Well, bully for you."

She shrugged and went off to the bedroom, leaving me standing there.

She always seems to win, whether she's in the right or not, and it drives me mad. If I'd stayed this late with my own boss, Tiffany, I'd be interrogated non-stop when I got back.

Of course, depending on how far I got with Tiffany, an interrogation might be a small price to pay.

~ ~ ~ ~ *April* ~ ~ ~ ~

We've been married three months now, and Grant's a lot better behaved than he used to be. But there are still times when he irritates.

Last night was typical. On Fridays I'm often late getting home, but because it was a bit later than usual, he

65

threw a tantrum. I don't bother arguing with him when he's in that sort of mood.

Actually, I'd been enjoying myself, so I didn't really care what he thought. On Fridays, we usually all go from the office to get a drink together, and it's fun socializing and unwinding. But once in a while, like last night, when everyone else has gone, I stay on with my boss in his office. It's a bit of fun, having an after-hours drink with him, and a little kiss and cuddle. And if decisions are being made that affect me, I make sure that things go the right way.

He's forever pushing me to have sex, but so far I've refused. I let him touch me and undo buttons and zips. He loves all that, but he assumes he'll go all the way eventually.

This morning, Grant seemed to have got over his bad mood, and was cheerful enough when he went off to the gym. Not long afterwards, Dawn came round. It's nice having my sister in the same apartment block.

"So April, we've got another family gathering coming up. Does Grant still hate them so much?"

"He'd rather be anywhere else, but he's no choice. Mother is still a bit annoyed with him, although I think that's not a big issue now, but he's nervous about being around our brothers."

"I'm not surprised, after the way Ben hurt him. His eye took ages to heal. Ben's always had a violent side, but I still don't see how he managed it, even with Frank's help. Grant's so strong and powerful, I can't see anyone getting the better of him."

"Well, they did. Caught him by surprise."

"But you forgave Ben?"

"He did it for the right reasons, so I can't be that angry with him."

"You've always been closer to Ben than I have anyway. I don't think I would have forgiven him."

Dawn knew about Ben and me, from when we were children, but she didn't know everything.

"Anyway, Dawn, how's Robin? I haven't seen much of him lately."

"He's fine. The only thing worrying me is that he seems to have gone off sex, and I don't know why."

"He was never that keen anyway, was he?"

"No, but he was always willing. And he'd play games if I wanted. But I'm still seeing that car dealer occasionally, and he's always got some bizarre ideas for us. He even makes me, … Mmm, maybe I'll keep that to myself."

I giggled. "Maybe Robin's seeing someone too, and it's wearing him out."

"I'd know if he was. But that's not to say he hasn't developed a crush on someone, that might make him less interested in me. Anyway, what about you? Had it with your boss yet?"

"No. And I don't think I will. Actually, if I were to have sex with anyone in the office, it would be Scott. It's tricky being his manager, but I know he's keen. Little things he's said, when we've been alone."

"Is he good-looking?"

"Very. He's mid-twenties, and looks like one of those clean-cut men you get in TV series."

"Sounds cute. But no competition for him?"

"He's got a steady girlfriend, and I've seen her picture. Believe me, there's no competition. I don't know what he sees in her."

"Well, you said that being married shouldn't stop you having boyfriends. But you haven't done much about it. So will Scott be the first?"

I smiled. "Yes, I think he will."

Then Dawn laughed. "Apart from the one you showered with on your honeymoon."

# 19

It's Saturday, and I'd had a good week, until last night. I'm used to her late Fridays, when she's out with that office crowd. But last week was way too late. Then last night she did it again. She didn't get home until one o'clock, and wouldn't explain or apologize. Then the usual argument, with me getting angry, and her sitting there so sweet and innocent, lying her way out of anything.

Perhaps I shouldn't get so stressed out. After all, we get on well enough, after three months married, and there'll always be some differences with any couple. And our love life is good enough, when she's in the mood. Even last night, she had the energy to make the first move.

The atmosphere was tense this morning, but by the evening it was back to normal, with us watching some stupid quiz show on the TV.

When it broke for an ad, she said, "Grant, my feet need washing."

I've got used to her little habits, and I don't mind washing her feet for her. But usually she asks more politely. She was beginning to sound like her mother.

I said, "So what? Do you want me to do something?"

She sat there, sweetness and light, and looked down at her feet. "I said my feet need washing."

There was no point arguing, as it would get nowhere. So I got a bowl of water, and the other things, and knelt down to start.

She bent down and kissed me on the cheek.

I like doing things for her, but she's irritating at times, the way she expects it. I start something off as a favor, and next thing, she takes it for granted, and I'm the guilty one if I don't respond.

So I washed and dried her pretty little feet, and smoothed talc onto them. As usual, she took no notice, with her attention fixed on the TV, now on some old movie about Romans and gladiators. It crossed my mind that she was behaving as a queen, in ancient Rome, with me as her servant, or even her slave.

We've another of those damned family gatherings coming up. Her mother is getting friendlier, but I'm still wary of her, especially while that maniac Ben's around. In fact, I'd be better off not being there, and avoid the chance of causing aggravation.

The only one in the family I really like is Dawn, and I see her often enough anyway. She's been to our apartment a couple of times when April's out, pretending that she didn't know. I don't mind, as she's good for my ego, giving me signals about what we might do. She jokes about me getting into bed with her, but I've told her it's impossible, being in the same block. There's no way we could get away with it with April and Robin around.

# 20

It was time to leave for the family gathering. Grant had been looking miserable, so I knew he wasn't looking forward to it. Not that I blame him. It's my family after all. And he avoids talking to Ben and Frank after what they did. But it's important to me, and so it should be for him. After all he's part of the family now.

"Grant, we need to be going soon, or we'll be late."

He hesitated, so I knew something was coming. "April, I think I'll miss this one. I don't enjoy them much, and I'm not feeling that well."

I felt his forehead. "You seem all right to me, and you haven't got a temperature. Come on, you'll be fine. And we won't stay late."

He sat down. "I've got a headache, and anyway I think it's better that I'm not there. I don't get on with most of them, and they've no interest in me. And you and Dawn spend all your time talking with the other women."

"But you have to come. If I went on my own, they'd all be asking where you were. And what could I say? It would look awful, as if you didn't care. Come on, it's not so bad there, and I'll make sure I don't leave you on your own too much."

"I really don't want to go. The whole thing's boring, and the last thing I want is to see your brothers again."

"But Grant, it's only once in a while. Please. It's not a lot to ask."

He sat there in silence. I thought for a minute that he was going to agree, but then he said, "No. I'm not going. If I say anything to your mother, it'll probably be taken wrongly, and then Ben will get his fists out. So I'd end up sitting there in silence. So you go, and make up some excuse. But I'm staying here."

"Grant, think of me. It puts me in a very difficult position. Can't you come, for me?"

He folded his arms, and stared ahead.

It was so annoying. As always, he was thinking only of himself.

I slammed the door as hard as I could when I left.


~ ~ ~ ~ *Grant* ~ ~ ~ ~


After April had gone, I got to thinking. If she was still upset when she got there, and told Ben that I'd let her down, those damned brothers could be back. I checked the front door was locked, and put the chain on, before I settled back in the living room. The TV programs were garbage, but there was some amateur sport on, and a bottle of beer made it passable. And anything was better than being at her mother's house.

I'd been watching for about an hour, when I heard a noise. I turned down the volume. Then a shuffling sound.

I jumped out of my chair. "Shit. They're here."

I reached for my cell phone.

"Damn." I'd left it in the hallway when I was checking the door.

They'd be coming through soon, but this time I'd be ready.

I picked up the poker from the fireside, and stood there waiting. The fire's an imitation, but the poker's real enough.

Then the sound of movement, and the door handle was turning.

There were three of them this time. Ben in the lead, then Frank and another man, big and stupid like Frank. One of their hillbilly cousins.

They shuffled into the room, watching me, as I backed to the wall, with the poker in hand.

The cousin laughed. "You're ready to fight, eh?"

They circled round and I moved along the wall into a corner.

"Ben, please leave. I've called the police, and they'll be here soon."

Smiling, but without a word, Ben held up my cell phone. Then he threw it across the room.

As I looked across, Frank lunged at me, but I swiveled round, to strike him with the poker. And I landed a good blow.

But Ben and the cousin jumped me, and I was down. Then Frank and the cousin flattened me out on the floor on my back, and Ben came to stand over me. Now he had the poker.

"My sister's been humiliated by you. I told you last time, when you disrespected mother, that if you are asked to do something, you do it. That goes as much for my sister."

I stuttered, "For God's sake, it was only that I didn't want to go to your family get-together."

"You don't understand yet, do you? What do I have to do to make you understand?"

To the others, he said, "Hold him tight."

Ben raised the poker, and felt the weight of it.

I knew what he was going to do. "Please, —"

He slammed it down into my left shin, and I shouted out in pain.

I wasn't able to look down, but I knew it was bleeding.

Ben looked thoughtful. Maybe that was all he was going to do.

Then he walked away, and returned a few minutes later with a dishcloth and a roll of duct tape.

"No, please don't. I understand now. I really do."

"You make too much noise, Grant."

He forced the cloth into my mouth. The taste was disgusting. Then he tore off a strip of tape, and sealed it over my mouth. He raised the poker again, and he started.

My other shin, and my thighs.

The pain was horrendous, and I wanted to scream out. It was like some horror movie, with Ben hitting me, and Frank and the cousin laughing.

Ben slammed it harder than ever into my chest. Still painful through the clothing, but not as bad as my shins. Both of them felt cold and damp, from the bleeding.

Finally he stood upright.

"I'd hit you in the balls, but then you'd be no use to her. Now remember what I told you. If sis or mother ever ask you to do something, you do it. No questions. No arguments. And when April gets back, I want you to apologize, and promise her you'll do whatever she asks in future. If you don't say that to her, I'll find out, and we'll be back for another lesson. Now so you remember …"

He swung one foot back.

I could see what he was going to do, and I shook my head for him to stop.

Then the foot came flying forward at my head. I turned to the side, and closed my eyes, before it made contact.

A searing pain, before I passed out.


When I came to, I was still on the floor. I pulled the tape away, and got the disgusting mess out of my mouth. In the hallway were bits of wood where they'd wrenched the chain off. But there was no damage to the door. So Ben had used a key. In the bathroom, I stripped off, and looked at the damage.

There were red marks everywhere he'd hit me, and my shins had drying blood on them. They were what hurt the most. And now I really did have a headache. The side of my head was hellish sore, where he'd kicked me.

I washed the blood off my legs, and dressed, then waited.

How the hell did I get into this situation? And how do I get out of it? Maybe the answer was to get April away from the family. Maybe back to Seattle. And if she won't do that? I won't take any more of this from Ben.

Next time he tries anything, I need to be better prepared.

It was as I expected when I got to mother's. She said nothing, but I could tell she was annoyed. Fortunately, the others were sympathetic, but it was so irritating to be put in this position. Dawn never had this sort of problem with Robin.

Ben was ready to comfort me, as always, and we went out back to talk.

"April, don't let him get you down. It's probably a stupid one-off. He can't want to embarrass you like this again."

"I don't know, Ben. When you taught him that lesson, I thought you'd overreacted. But now I'm wondering if you didn't go far enough. He's so awkward with me sometimes, arguing about anything, and yet I try my hardest to be reasonable. He's so beastly to me at times, and it's not fair."

I could feel my tears were forming, and I dabbed them with a tissue.

He put his arm round me. "He's no right to upset you this way. I'm going to go and see him."

I only wanted some sympathy, and hadn't thought of Ben going round there now. But, on the other hand, Grant shouldn't get off scot-free.

"Ben, if you do go to see him, can you just talk to him? You hurt him so much last time. Promise you won't hit him."

"He needs to understand what harm he's doing. I can't make that promise."

"At least promise you won't hit his face again. You almost damaged his eye you know."

"Shall I go and see him or not?"

I didn't really want Grant to get hurt again, but something had to be done. Why should I be the one upset, with him sitting around at home without a care?

I kissed Ben on the cheek, and gave him the key.

When I got home, Grant was subdued.

He asked, "How was it there without me?"

"It wasn't too bad. Everyone seemed to understand."

He went quiet for a moment. "April, I've got something to say. I'm sorry for refusing to go with you. I know these things are important to you."

"So you'll come next time?"

"Darling, from now on, if you ask me to do something, I'll do it. And no argument."

"Oh that's marvelous. I'd hate to have to go on my own again. And you'll do anything I ask? You can't mean that."

"Every word."

"I might ask you to do silly things."

It was the first time I'd felt cheerful today. I thought carefully. What would I really like? I suppose it would be nice to be pampered a little. I'd make it sound bossy.

"Grant, go and get me a glass of wine."

He smiled, and went off.

I sat in the chair opposite the TV, and tried a few channels. There was nothing on, so I switched to a shopping channel. I could watch them for hours, but Grant hates them.

He came back with the wine, and handed it to me.

"Grant, darling, can you take my shoes off? It's been a long day, and a little massage would be nice."

It was heaven. The shopping channel, sipping wine, while he was down there looking after my feet.

After a few minutes, I leaned down and kissed him on the cheek. "You're a perfect husband. Now go to the bedroom, and get undressed, then lie on the bed and wait for me. I'll be along in a while, and maybe we'll have a little fun."

Off he went, and he couldn't stop smiling.

I was in no rush. I got another glass of wine, and watched more shopping. He'd been waiting for a half-hour by the time I entered the bedroom.

The marks on his legs were awful. Ben had been rough with him. But thankfully not on his face, where it showed, although there did seem to be some sort of lump behind his ear. And now Grant was behaving perfectly.

I undressed slowly in front of him. In the mirror, I looked so small and delicate compared to him lying there with all his muscles. But I was the one in control.

I went over and got onto the bed with him.

He put his arm around me, and then a hand on my breast. It didn't take long for him to get aroused. Then his hand moved downwards. He's a bit clumsy, but I'm used to it.

Then he must have judged that I was ready, or at least that he was. He got up, put a condom on, and then back on the bed, he knelt over me.

He was excited, and getting ready to put it into me. Now I'd have some fun.

I said, "Darling, let's do something different tonight."

He answered quickly, so I knew it had his interest. "What do you want me to do?"

I put my bossy voice on, well as bossy as I can sound. "Get that vibrator out."

"But I'm ready for sex now, aren't you?"

I stayed silent. In the end, he reached down to get it from the cupboard.

I spread my arms and legs out. I could have felt vulnerable, but I didn't. Those marks on his legs made the difference.

"Grant, use it on me, but gently."

He pushed the tip of it into me, and I jumped. "It's cold."

He laughed. "Sorry, I'll warm it with my hands."

"No, warm it in your mouth. That'll be better."

He shrugged, and put it into his mouth.

It was quite erotic looking up at him. After a few seconds, I said, "You look like you're sucking a penis."

He pulled it out quickly, his face flushed.

Then it was back into me, and it was warm now. I closed my eyes, and he pushed it gently in, and started the vibrations. It was lovely lying there, not having to do anything or to look excited when I wasn't. It was like being at a spa, and having the staff do all the work, while I relaxed.

Then he turned up the speed. I could feel the throbbing deep inside me, so strong it was almost painful. He must have deliberately turned it to the maximum to get me to say something. I was going to stop him, but then I began getting used to it. My body was absorbing it, and responding to it. All I could think of now was this throbbing inside me, and the pleasure it gave me.

I knew my orgasm was coming, but when it did come, it was more violent than I expected.

My body shook, and I screamed out.

It was some minutes before I could breathe properly again. "Grant, that was so erotic. You did it perfectly."

He leaned over me and kissed me. "I'm still in the mood for sex. Maybe in a little while?"

I gave him my best smile. He still had an erection, but that wasn't my problem.

"Don't be silly, that's enough for one night."

He looked disappointed. But it was important that he learn his lesson. Then I had an idea.

"And darling, I want to sleep on my own tonight. I want to spread out in the bed, and remember what you did for me."

"But we always sleep together."

"One more kiss, then off you go. You can use the guest bedroom."

I thought he was going to say something. His mouth started to open. But then he kissed me and left.

I lay on my back, and spread out my arms and legs again.

It was so luxurious having the bed all to myself.

It had been a bad start to the day, but it had ended perfectly.

# 21

After the events of yesterday, April and I had a reasonable day together. Driving to shopping centers and wandering around malls isn't my favorite activity, but April loved it, and it was good to be together. We stopped at a diner for lunch, and chatted about this and that, avoiding mention of the family.

Then she dropped it on me.

"Grant, darling, did you sleep well last night?"

"Yes, fine. I'd rather have been with you though."

"I slept wonderfully. You do move around a lot at night, and it sometimes wakes me up. It was so much more restful being on my own."

"Are you saying you want separate beds?"

"No, not exactly. I enjoy sleeping with you, but it doesn't have to be every night. So I want to try something. When we're back, I'll move your clothes into the guest room, and that can become your room. Then it's going to be easier if we want to sleep together one night or not, as we wish. It makes it more flexible."

"So what about tonight?"

"That's what I meant. We should try sleeping apart, but then sleep together when we feel like it."

"It makes it awkward having sex, doesn't it?"

"Not at all. If I'm in the mood, you can come to me."

"And then go back to my room?"

She smiled. "That depends on how we both feel afterwards. You know, I think it could be fun."

It wasn't my idea of fun. But she'd made her mind up. Anyway I didn't want to make a scene, as I had something else to ask her about.

78

"You know, April, I've been looking at the job market, and there are some great opportunities back in Seattle, for both of us. A lot more pay than we're getting round here."

"Salaries might be higher, but there's quality of life to think about. Anyway, we've enough money, haven't we?"

"I suppose so, but I'm bored with my job. It's not got the excitement of aerospace, and I'm ready for a change. If we moved —"

She interrupted me, "Anyway, we can't leave Oregon. My family's here."

I'd already anticipated that. "But we can visit easily enough."

"No, Grant, I love my family, and I don't want to only have occasional visits. I have to live here."

So far what I expected. Now for my compromise.

"I suppose I could take a job in Seattle, Monday to Friday, and be back here weekends?"

She looked aghast. "That would be like separating. We couldn't do that. We're married and we'll be together, till death us do part, if you recall. I don't remember it only being weekends."

So there was going to be no compromise. If I ever did leave Portland, I'd be going alone. And I'd have to be ready for Ben and his friends coming after me.

I'd need something more than a poker.

# Part 5 – OFFICE SEX AND DOMESTIC VIOLENCE

## 22

*~ ~ ~ ~ April ~ ~ ~ ~*

Things are so much better now, with Grant having his own room.

It's been two weeks, and I love sleeping alone, yet knowing he's nearby to look after me. I'm sleeping better, and I'm sure it's having an effect on my complexion. I told Dawn, but she says I'm imagining it. Anyway, we'll see who's right as time goes by.

Dawn's intrigued, so I told her to try it with Robin. It's not that simple, as they haven't got a spare bedroom, so he'd be on the couch. But she says he's no trouble anyway. Perhaps he doesn't pester her, the way Grant does when we're in bed.

I've invited Grant twice to sleep with me. He's been so anxious to please, and I've really enjoyed it. And it's more erotic having sex that way. It makes it special each time, like a lover coming to me in the night.

The first time, I let Grant stay the night afterwards, but the second time, I told him he was to come in at midnight, and not say anything, but make love to me, then leave. I imagined it was the stripper from my bachelor party, come to seduce me. That was really exciting.

But tonight I expect to be doing something else altogether. The company is having a corporate off-site today, and my boss got me an invite. It's not everyone on my level who's going, and there's a lot of discussion of why some people were invited, and others not. I feel quite privileged, so I'll have a favor to return.

"Will you be all right tonight, Grant? I've got a lasagna for you in the fridge, and you can watch all the sports you want."

"I still don't see why you're staying the night downtown. Surely it's easy enough to come home afterwards?"

"I can't do that. We're working through the day and into the evening, and everyone is expected to stay at the hotel. Then there's a breakfast meeting to recap on the work done. It would look ridiculous to go home, and then come back next morning."

"Okay, whatever you say. I suppose it's mostly men there?"

"I know two other women are going, but that's probably it. It's an old-fashioned organization, so it's hardly surprising."

"Well, I'll be here if you need me."

I'd driven off to the hotel, feeling nervous. It was an important event, and I'd be getting to know some senior people. Who knows where that could lead? But by the afternoon, I was tired of the whole thing. We were expected to work on a mission statement and everyone there was posturing, trying to make an impression on the top brass.

By the time we got to have dinner, I was pleased to see an end to it. Just as well there was no evening session. But dinner was fine. I had two of the senior executives either side of me, and we got on well. One of them even touched my knee under the table. Accidentally no doubt.

After dinner, it was exactly what I'd expected. To my manager's room for a nightcap and whatever else he had in mind. He'd already had too much to drink, and wouldn't be much use. But I owed it to him, for getting me the invite. And I'd kept him at bay long enough.

I'd packed a sheer pink nightie, as a treat for him, but in his state it didn't seem worth bothering.

So into bed, with some clumsy groping, and then he was on top of me. The whole thing can't have lasted ten minutes. Brief and unexciting, but he went to sleep happy, and that's what matters.

I suppose that's what prostitutes do. It's awful to think that they do that for money, and even with men they find unpleasant. I lay there a long time looking at him lying asleep. Nothing like Grant's physique, but pretty good shape for his age. I'm lucky really. My faithful husband, back home, and me here with the freedom to experiment. I fell asleep with the light on.

It was five o'clock when I woke, and still dark. He looked so content lying there. He'd done a lot for me, and I'd hardly repaid him.

I got out of bed, put on the nightie, fluffed my hair, and touched up my lipstick.

I'll wake him up, then we'll see what he can do.

# 23

April came with me to the gym yesterday. I didn't know why, until we got there, but she wanted to see my trainer.

"Would you say that Grant's got a perfect physique?"

"He's about as good as it gets, without getting obsessive, and the weight training is keeping him in shape." He looked at me. "But we'll have to make sure he keeps it up."

"Is there anything else he can do to build his muscles?"

"He could spend more time here, but there's a limit."

"What about supplements?"

I interrupted, "I'm taking extra protein already. I can't take any more, or I'll be sick of it."

"What about what those sportsmen take? Steroids isn't it?"

The trainer laughed. "Well, yes, that would work. But they're not something to mess with, and they're banned from sports all around the world."

"Well Grant's not going to be competing in anything. So that's not an issue."

"Actually, they're technically illegal too. You can't go to the corner store for them. And you wouldn't want to tell people that you're using them."

"But you could get them?"

He looked around, as if to reassure himself. "Yes. But they're expensive."

I said, "Hold on, April, I'm not sure I want to start taking that stuff. There are side effects."

"What sort of side effects?"

The trainer said, "Well, they act like testosterone, if you know what I mean, and I don't think Grant needs any more of that."

She smiled. "Then that's not a problem. We'll pay the going rate. So when can you get them?"

It was a relief to be at work, without more of April's bright ideas. Why she wanted me to build yet more muscle, I didn't know. And the last thing I needed was more testosterone, what with her sleeping in the next room.

I must have been looking worried, as Tiffany came over. She's not a bad boss, for a woman, but she does think too much about our welfare. She asked if I had a problem, and I laughed it off, but she insisted that we get out of there, and go for lunch.

There's a Mexican cafe near where we work, and it was refreshing to be there, in the outdoor area, eating enchiladas, and drinking root beer.

"So Grant, do you want to talk about it? I'm a good listener."

"I wouldn't want to trouble you. It's just that April and I have our differences. I love her and I know she loves me, so I suppose that's the main thing. But her attitude's strange, at least that's the way I see it."

"For example?"

"She's got me sleeping in a separate room. Said she wanted to try it for a while, but it's beginning to look permanent."

"So you two aren't, you know, …"

"Oh, we get together occasionally. Not as often as I'd like, but that's not the problem."

"Then what is? Being apart?"

"Tiffany, it's more than that. Sometimes I feel I'm just an accessory for her. She likes having me around, and having me with her when we're out. But she sometimes treats me as a servant, and sometimes as if I'm her pet dog."

I shut up then. Tiffany was looking anxious, and I'd probably said too much. My hands were on the table, and she reached across and put her hands on mine.

"I don't know what to say, Grant. If I could help, I would. You're special to me, you know that."

It was good to feel her touch, and see her concern. "It's been a help talking to you. There's nothing else that you can do though. I've got to work things out for myself."

She gave my hands a squeeze. "Well, I'm here for you, if you need me. Don't forget that."

It seemed to be an invitation, but I couldn't be sure. That would be great, to be accused of unwanted sexual advances to my manager. But it did seem to be an invitation.

So I was in a good mood until I got home, and found Ben there. We made conversation for a while. But I wanted him out of there, and he knew it.

Finally he stood up. "I'll have to go now. Thanks for the coffee."

He got to the door, and April went with him. I could see their reflection in the hallway mirror.

"Goodbye Ben, thanks for coming round."

Then she kissed him. On his lips.

When she came back into the room, I asked, "So Ben's been here a while?"

"Yes, I had the afternoon off, so I invited him over for coffee."

"What did you find to talk about? Me, I suppose?"

"Oh, mostly it was family things. But I did tell him he'd been too violent with you. Those awful marks on your legs."

"What did he say to that?"

"He said he was doing it for me, and got carried away. He does care a lot for me, you know."

I had to ask. "When you kissed him goodbye, was that on the lips?"

She hesitated. "Yes, what about it?"

"Oh nothing."

It seemed odd to me, kissing her brother that way. And not a brief touch.

More like a lover's kiss.

# 24

We'd finished breakfast, and we were both ready to head off to work, when I remembered.

"Grant, that new movie's showing now, the one I told you about."

"Isn't that another chick flick?"

"It's got romance, if that's what you mean."

"The last one you took me to was boring. People talking endlessly about their relationships. I can't understand how these movies do so well."

"It's because they're well made, and they appeal to lots of people. Anyway, I thought we might go this evening, after work."

He sighed. "I'll come with you if you want. But don't expect me to enjoy it."

He could be so infuriating. "You'll spoil it with that attitude. It was bad enough last time with your tutting and yawning."

"I can't help it getting bored with that touchy-feely stuff, especially when there's no action. If you looked around, there weren't many men in the audience. Those movies are designed for women."

"Well, I'll go on my own then. At least I'll be with people who want to be there."

I got away from the office promptly and was home before Grant. A quick snack, then I could concentrate on getting ready.

By the time he arrived, I was dressed to kill. Cocktail dress, necklace, high heels. I looked pretty good.

I came through to the kitchen, where he was getting a beer from the fridge.

"I've eaten already, Grant, so you'll have to find something yourself. I'm off to the movies."

"You look glamorous. Why all that for the movies? It was jeans and trainers last time."

"If you must know, I'm meeting up with one of my staff from the office. Unlike you, Scott's keen to see it. So I said I'd take him for a late drink afterwards."

"Who's Scott? I haven't heard you mention him before."

"He didn't work for me before, that's why. He's a hard worker and that's what counts."

"How old is he?"

"He's mid-twenties. And that's enough questions. I'll go and check my make-up, and then I've to rush. I'm collecting him from his apartment. It's the least I can do."

"So what time will you be back?"

"How would I know? The movie's a couple of hours, and then we've drinks. We might be there a while, if we find enough to talk about. And then I've to take him home. So don't stay up."

Grant was sullen. "It sounds as if you're going on a date."

My first thought was to deny it, or laugh it off. But why should I? Why lie about it? And it even makes me feel excited to think of saying it.

"That's right. I've got a date with Scott."


It was two o'clock by the time I got back home, and Grant had gone to bed. In these circumstances, it makes it so much easier to have my own room.

As I lay in bed, my mind was too busy for sleep. Scott had been fun, and he liked the movie as much as me. We laughed at the same things, and when I cried at the end, he put his arm round me, and let my head rest on his shoulder. The drink in the bar afterwards was enjoyable too. It's nice to get to know each other, outside of the office. He told me about himself, and I told him a little about myself. We're really quite compatible.

If I were to have a boyfriend, then Scott would be a good candidate. He didn't actually say he was keen on me, but I knew he was, from the questions he asked, trying to find out whether I'd have an affair outside marriage, and how I felt about him. I kept things vague, and that seemed to get him even more interested in me. I'll never understand men. You make yourself hard to get, and that makes them want you all the more.

When I took him back to his apartment, he invited me in for a coffee.

But as soon as we were in the door, he wanted to kiss me. I pretended to be reluctant, and it was driving him crazy. So when I said he could, it was as if he'd been let out of a trap, and we were soon embracing and kissing. He's got very sensuous hands.

We never even got past the hallway, standing there, caressing each other. It really did feel like I'd been on a date, with the end-of-evening kissing.

He whispered to me, "April, let's go the bedroom."

"Scott, you're wicked. We can't do that. I know what that would lead to."

"And? What's wrong with that?"

"Well, for a start, it wouldn't really be fair on Grant."

I said it hesitantly, without conviction.

"He's never going to know."

"But I'd know. Anyway, what about your girlfriend? It would be unfair on her too, and, I don't know why, but that seems worse to me."

"But she'd never know either. So what's the harm in having some fun together?"

I frowned, to show I was struggling with the answer.

"I've loved having a date with you, and I'd like to do it again. And it might be a perfect ending to go to bed with you. But I can't do it while you have a girlfriend. I know it might not be rational, but that's it. That's the way I feel."

He kissed me good night at the door as I left, looking preoccupied.

He'll dump her soon, so as to be ready for our next date.

Then I'll be his new girlfriend.

# 25

April's gone off for the weekend, for another off-site. She was excited about it, and said it's a big deal for her career, but she tells me that every time she puts work first. This one's in San Diego, and she won't be back until Monday evening.

Saturdays aren't bad on my own, as there's plenty of sport to watch in the day, and I get out to the gym. But the evenings are boring, so it was good of Dawn and Robin to invite me round for dinner.

Dawn and I were in the living room, with Robin busy as usual in the kitchen.

"So how's married life, Grant?"

"It's okay. Not quite what I expected, but okay."

"That's not very enthusiastic for a man not even married a year. My sister not making a good wife?"

"April's fine, but she's some attitudes that annoy me. Especially when she feels like ordering me around."

"But you knew she was like that before you married."

"I didn't realize how extreme she is about it. Sometimes she talks to me as if I'm her servant."

I could have said that it was the same way Dawn treats Robin, but I've more sense than that.

"So what else isn't working the way you expected?"

"I'm sorry to say it, Dawn, but your family is part of the problem. Your mother just about tolerates me, but aside from you and Robin, I don't get along much with the rest of them. Yet I have to go to these family meetings all the same."

"Well, you can't change the family. April and I grew up with them, and we don't have a problem. And Robin copes well enough."

I was going to say something about Ben, but then I thought better of it. Who knows what Dawn might repeat to others, even to Ben?

I changed topic, "Anyway, at least you're there, and we get along fine."

She smiled. "It's because I like you, Grant. I like you a lot —"

Robin called out. Dinner was ready.

Robin was talkative while we ate. He works in a biology lab, and they're on the brink of some discovery that he found exciting. The more he told us about it, the less interesting it seemed.

My attention was on Dawn anyway. While Robin chattered away, she'd given me some furtive smiles, and at one point, I felt her foot touching the side of my leg. My mind was occupied until I realized that Robin had asked me about my own job.

"It's pretty good. Similar work to what I did in Seattle, but more free time."

"And the people there?"

My immediate thought was of Tiffany. "They're a good crowd. Even the senior management seem regular people. Yes, the job's a good one. Of course, I don't get these off-sites like April. Especially to San Diego."

Dawn said, "She told me it's mostly very senior people, so she thinks she's on a fast track. Her boss might be leaving soon, and I think she's angling for his job this weekend."

"I'd rather she was at home, but I don't mind her going. It's only fair that she pursues her career."

And at least she wouldn't be on any more dates with Scott.

Robin had taken the dishes away, and was busy again in the kitchen.

Dawn topped up her wine, and asked, "And you sleep separately now?"

So April had told her. It was bad enough already without her telling her sister.

"Yes, most of the time."

Robin came back in.

Dawn said, "I wouldn't want that. I don't sleep well on my own."

So Robin knew too. Probably the whole damned neighborhood knew.

"It's not so bad. April sleeps better on her own."

Dawn said, "Shall I tell you a secret about Robin?"

Robin's face went pink. Dawn had had too much booze, and it was time to go. I didn't want to know their secrets.

I looked at my watch. "Hell, I've overstayed my welcome. I'd better get back to my place."

She ignored me. "I have Robin pretend to be a woman sometimes."

I didn't know what to say. But then, if Robin knew something about my predicament, maybe it was only fair I knew something about his. I looked at Robin. "Really?"

He didn't answer. Dawn said, "Robin, go and put your wig on, and show Grant."

He said, "Grant wouldn't be interested."

She looked at me. "You would, wouldn't you?"

She didn't wait for an answer. "Robin, go and put it on. Go on. And your lipstick."

He shuffled off, and I sat there waiting, with Dawn sipping her wine.

When he came back, he was wearing a fluffy blonde wig, with hair down to his shoulders. And bright red lipstick. Those two things transformed his appearance.

"Robin, it's amazing. I hardly recognize you."

He looked embarrassed, but pleased too.

Dawn looked on him proudly. "With a nightie on, and in low light, he looks like a woman. We have some fun then, don't we Robin."

Now he looked embarrassed again. He smiled politely at me, then took the wig off. He smoothed the hair on the wig, and then did the same with his own hair.

"She wants variety. It's hard for me to keep up with her sometimes."

Dawn said to me, "I think sex is dull if you don't experiment. Don't you agree?"

But she didn't wait for an answer.

She stood up. "I'm feeling dizzy. I'll have to go and lie down." And wandered off, leaving me with Robin.

I said, "Hey, I'm sorry if I embarrassed you. Dawn doesn't seem to mind what she talks about."

"I'm used to it, so no need to apologize. I don't mind anyway if it's you and April."

"You know, it makes me wonder about April. I don't know how the conversation got round to it, but she'd asked me the other day if I thought she'd make a good dominatrix."

Robin laughed. "She's hardly the type."

"That's what I said. I told her she was too cute for that kind of thing. She got really annoyed with me, and I wasn't sure why. Hell, she must know what she looks like."

Robin frowned. "But maybe she's looking for variety too, and thought of that as one way?"

"She's not said. But maybe I'll have to think about it. And Robin, can you take that lipstick off? It's distracting."

He pouted at me, and it made me smile.

# 26

I was tired when I got home on Monday evening.

Grant was standing with the front door ajar when I got there, and I thought at first it was a confrontation he had in mind, but he was smiling.

"Come in, April. I've got something special for you."

We went on through to the living room, where he had a bottle of champagne, with two glasses, and a little banner on the wall, "Welcome Home".

He can be so sweet at times. I sat down with him and sipped the champagne.

"This is a lot of fuss. I've only been away two days."

"I know. But you deserved a treat. You've been working so hard."

"That's true, but I think it's going to pay off. My boss is leaving, and I've been told informally that the job is mine. They liked the way I handled the last downsizing, and it sounds as if there's more of that on the way."

"But don't you have interviews and selection panels, that kind of thing?"

"Oh, yes, I'll have to go through that. It's a nuisance, but the company regulations insist on it, and we have to be sure that no one can say afterwards that there wasn't due process."

"But you'll definitely be getting the job?"

"Well, I've done enough to be fairly sure."

He laughed. "Did that include getting friendly with your boss?"

"As a matter of fact, it did. But nothing you need worry about."

"No sex, then?"

I'd wondered about confessing to Grant how far I'd gone, to see his reaction, and each time, I talked myself out of it. However, he's the one that's raised the subject.

I lowered my eyes. "I can't lie to you. Yes, he did have sex with me one time."

We sat in silence. I was waiting for him to explode, but the silence was almost worse.

I said, "I'm sorry, Grant. It was at that first off-site. I was silly enough to drink too much, and he took advantage of me. It's as simple as that. The next morning he didn't mention it, and I'm not sure he even remembered. I think he'd been more drunk than me."

Silence again.

"Grant, aren't you going to say anything?"

"I'm disappointed, that's all. How would you feel if I was saying it to you?"

"I suppose I'd feel the same. But if it wasn't your fault, then I'd understand."

"So what happened this weekend?"

"Nothing like that. I'd learned my lesson, and kept to a cocktail and a couple of glasses of wine. But he wasn't there anyway, and no one else behaves that way. These senior executives are gentlemen."

That wasn't quite true. My boss was there all right, but for me he was history anyway, with him moving on. My sights were on a vice-president now. And I don't much care if he's a gentleman or not.

Grant was silent again, then said. "I went round to Dawn's for dinner on Saturday."

It was a relief that he changed the subject. So I've admitted adultery, and got away with it. A lot easier than I expected.

"I presume Robin was there too?"

Grant paused. "Some of the time."

It was so obvious that he was trying to get me jealous.

"So did Dawn make a pass at you?"

"No, we just talked. She had quite a lot to drink. It seems you've told her about us sleeping separately."

"It's nothing we need to hide. Lots of couples do it."

He smiled. "She got Robin embarrassed at one point. Said how she has him pretend to be a woman for their sex games."

"Oh, I know about that, and I don't agree with it. He's effeminate enough, without that kind of thing. If she keeps dressing him up, he'll end up gay."

"I hope you don't ever want me to do that."

I burst out laughing. "No way. You'd look ridiculous. And I want you the way you are. My prize bull."

I kissed him, but he looked miserable. He needed a reward, poor thing.

"Grant, you can sleep with me tonight. And no role-playing like Robin. You can be yourself."


~ ~ ~ ~ *Grant* ~ ~ ~ ~


At work, I was busy all morning with a rush job, and having to concentrate. But I couldn't stop thinking about April. She'd told me she'd had sex with her boss, as if it was unimportant. And I'd let it go by without an argument, not knowing what to say. Anyone else but her would have kept it secret, but she told me openly. Then she let me sleep with her, as if that solved everything. She's impossible.

I was late for lunch in the staff cafeteria, so ate alone. I was so deep in thought that Tiffany caught me by surprise when she sat down opposite.

"That was good work, Grant. It's gone down well that we got that finished."

I smiled politely.

She leaned forward. "What's the matter? You look as miserable as sin. Was it that stressful this morning?"

"Oh, it's nothing here. It's married life I suppose. It doesn't help that April's not home half the time. She had a long weekend away, and now she's got some meeting this evening. I won't see her until midnight, and I'll be eating some microwave crap while she's having a four-star dinner."

Tiffany laughed. That always makes her eyes sparkle. "Well, I can't promise anything four-star, but you're welcome to come to my place after work, and I can fix you something."

"No, I'll be all right. No point burdening you with my moods."

"Nonsense. I won't take no for an answer. After work, my place, and that's an order from your manager. Okay?"

I smiled. "Okay. Order understood."

She was right about the meal. A pizza delivery wasn't four-star, but it was the best meal I'd had for a few days, and with a couple of beers, the most fun for longer than that.

Tiffany was different too, out of the workplace. She'd let her hair down, and changed into a thin blouse and skin-tight black leggings.

Maybe she planned it, but I don't think so. I think it's the way things happen. Lately I've been wanting even more sex, just when I've been getting less from April, and at times, I'm almost desperate. I blame it on those steroids, but whatever the reason, in my current state, I'd have any sex that was available.

But with my manager? Probably breaks a dozen company rules.

But April did it, so why shouldn't I?

"Tiffany, why don't you come over here?"

She jumped onto the sofa next to me. "Yes?"

I took hold of her hands, and held them for a while, looking into her eyes. "You know what I want to do now, don't you?"

"Let me guess."

She kissed me. "Was that what you wanted, or was it something else?"

I pulled her close, and kissed her again, running my hand down her back, feeling the shape of her body, past her waist, down to her hips.

Now I had to have her.

# 27

It's going to be interesting this evening. A company social event for the managers in the Operations division, and their spouses. My favorite VP will be there, making the opening speech.

I've got the interview next week for my boss's old job, and there are rumors everywhere who might be chosen. What I find delightful is that no one thinks I'm in the running. There are four other candidates, and one of them is an all-American type, tall and rugged, with one of those really deep voices. He coaches school soccer, and goes to church regularly, and with four kids and a trophy wife, he's considered the front-runner. It's going to be sweet beating him to the job. That's real girl power.

Most of the managers are men, so the spouses will no doubt be a bunch of bitchy women. There's only one other woman manager, and she's divorced, so Grant's going to be the only male spouse. He's looking forward to the session after dinner, where we break up, with the managers in one room, and spouses in another.

"Are you ready yet, Grant?"

"Yes. And your boss definitely won't be there?"

"No. He's gone."

"Good. I might have gone and popped him one on the chin."

I went up to him and straightened his tie. "You're awful, Grant. Now best behavior tonight. I'm in line for that job, but don't say a word."

I hadn't told him that Scott would be there. Until yesterday, he wasn't to be going, as his position is short of what qualifies him to attend. But they've had some cancellations, and he was on a reserve list, as high-potential. I'll have to be careful.

It turned out to be boring, apart from my networking with the execs. Grant got on fine, even with Scott. God only knows what they talked about. Probably me. I hope Scott was careful what he said.

When it came to an end, poor Scott had been drinking too much, and was worried about driving, so I suggested he come and stay the night with us.

Back home, Scott went off to sleep in the spare room, leaving me and Grant having a late coffee.

I said, "You seemed to get on with everyone there. Did you enjoy it?"

"Actually I did. I wasn't expecting it to be interesting, but they're a good lot of people. I can see why you like working there."

"And what about your session with the spouses?"

"That was a joke. The host wasn't expecting a man. So his script was comical. About us spouses helping our husbands' careers, and networking with one another about recipes and childcare. I was at the back, and he looked over at me every now and then, waiting for some adverse comment. But I was good, and kept my mouth closed."

"Did you have a chance to chat with the wives?"

Grant smiled. "A few yes. Even the wife of the VP."

"She's so old-fashioned, isn't she?"

"She's nice. Actually I meant to ask you something. She said there was some trouble with an ex-employee. Threatening company staff, and you included."

"It's the man I made redundant. He ought to move on and get another job, instead of making trouble for everyone."

"But have you been threatened?"

I couldn't tell Grant everything, otherwise his macho side would have him driving off to find the man. Then heaven knows what would happen.

"No, not personally. He's been more about trying to sabotage the company's reputation, but he won't get anywhere doing that. Social media or not, he'll never get enough people interested in what happened to him. And believe me, we did everything by the book, so he won't get anywhere with the courts."

"I met some others too, managers and wives. Those our age seemed the most interesting."

"I think there are certain people there that we could get to know better, after this ice-breaker. Does that sound a good idea?"

"Sure."

This would be tricky. So I'd have to go gently.

"And then you wouldn't need to go and see Harry and those other people in Seattle."

Grant looked puzzled. "But they're friends."

"I know that, darling, but we have to move on. They can't do us any good there, but with the right contacts here, it'll all be good for my career."

"I notice you don't want to meet my work colleagues."

"It's hardly the same thing. Your career isn't going anywhere, is it? So what would be the point?"

As soon as I said it, I regretted it. It was true enough, but I still shouldn't have said it.

Grant said, "That's unfair. It's an interesting job, and pays well enough, and the people there respect me. We don't all need to have a career planned out."

"I know that, and I'm sorry. I didn't mean to upset you. All I'm saying is that in your job, you do good work, and everyone's happy, but that's it. If you try and network and do what I do, it's not going to make any difference. But in my job, the opportunities are there for advancement, and it would be silly to pass them by."

"I suppose so. Anyway, I'm ready for bed. What about we sleep together tonight?"

I smiled. "Nice thought, but I'm tired. Maybe tomorrow night."

Grant seems obsessed with sex lately. If it's those steroids, then maybe he'll have to come off them. A shame though, because his chest and arms look better than ever.

Anyway, I didn't want sex with him tonight. Not with Scott in the house, a few yards away.

# 28

It's been two weeks since I had sex with April. She's always putting me off, and it's getting me down. And it's Sunday tomorrow, with the goddamn family meeting, so there'll be no chance of anything after that.

I've been wondering about getting together with Tiffany again, but it's tricky. At work, we have to stay formal, and she's not shown any signs that she wants to see me again after-hours. I think she's keen, but one of us needs to make the first move.

April switched off the TV. "Grant, will you take your shirt and pants off?"

"Why?"

"I want to look at you, that's all."

I took them off, and stood in front of her in my briefs. She stood up, and walked around me, looking me over, as if I was something she might be buying.

She reached out and touched my chest. "Those steroids are working. Your muscles are definitely firmer. Have you put on weight?"

"About six pounds I think."

"Well, it shows. You're a real hunk, and I like that. Now how about you stay undressed, and give my feet a massage?"

She sat down, kicked off her slippers, and stretched her feet out.

I knelt down, and took hold of one foot.

She said, "Don't be silly, you need to wash them first."

So up again, and then back with a bowl and the rest of it, to wash them.

She switched the TV back on, to a quiz show, while I washed and dried, and rubbed on the talc. She does have beautiful feet. It's a pleasure handling them.

Then finally I got to her massage. I don't know why, but I found it very erotic doing that. As I stroked and squeezed her feet, I was getting an erection, and my briefs felt tight on me.

When she'd had enough, she tapped me on the shoulder and I stood up.

She stared at my briefs. "My God, Grant, have you been adding muscle there too?"

She reached out and touched me, and giggled.

"It's a pity I don't want sex tonight, you must really be in the mood."

"We haven't slept together for ages. What do you expect?"

She frowned. "I'm sorry, but I have to be in the mood for sex too. But I might let you sleep with me. And I might even give you a little massage."

"Hell, April, if you do that, I'll ejaculate."

"Well, you'd better have a condom on then."


~ ~ ~ ~ *April* ~ ~ ~ ~


When I came back from the bathroom, Grant was standing there, waiting for me. He looked even better, stripped off altogether. He really has a beautiful body.

And I look pretty good too. I went and stood next to him, and looked in the mirror.

"Don't we look handsome, Grant? Both perfect bodies."

His penis had calmed down now. Even so, it seemed bigger than it used to be. So maybe the steroids do work down there too.

He smiled. "We'd look even better if we have sex in front of the mirror."

103

We'd done that before, and I loved it. But he has to know that once I've made a decision, he should accept it.

"It's a nice idea, but I told you I didn't want sex tonight. We can lie together, and play a little. So come on, let's do that, and then we'll get some sleep."

I switched off the lights and got into bed, and he followed. His hands were soon on me. For such a big man, he can be quite gentle at times.

I put my hand across to his penis. Erect again, I could feel the muscles and veins bulging out. He'd got himself really worked up, without much help from me. So I took my hand away.

He said, "April, let's make love. Please. We've not done it for so long."

"Not tonight. I told you that, so stop suggesting it. Now it's time to sleep."

I kissed him, and turned away from him. But he moved up behind me, and put his arm round to feel my breast.

"Grant, stop that."

He ignored me. He's been so well-behaved recently, but now he was becoming irritating.

"Grant, I told you. Let go of me, and get to sleep."

He kept on, squeezing my breasts harder, and it was getting uncomfortable.

I turned round to face him, and said as firmly as I could, "Stop it. I've had enough."

Then he went crazy.

He got up onto his knees, above me, and grabbed hold of my shoulders and shook me like I weighed nothing. "I'm not stopping. I'm going to fuck you."

I tried fighting back, but he lowered himself onto me, crushing me, and I felt him forcing his way in, much too quickly. And it was painful.

I mumbled, "No, please, don't. You're hurting me."

But he wouldn't stop. My small body was being shaken and abused, and he didn't care. It probably didn't matter that it was me. Any woman would have done.

When I struggled against him, it made him more violent. So I gave up, and lay there until he'd had enough.

When he finally came off me, I was able to breathe properly again. His behavior was inexcusable, and I felt violated. I wanted to shout at him, but what could I say that would make any difference? The beast in him had enjoyed it, and he wouldn't regret it no matter what I said.

So it was silence for a while. Then he got out of bed, and went to his room, without a word.

He must learn never to do that again. He had to be punished.

~ ~ ~ ~ *Grant* ~ ~ ~ ~

That was quite something with April last night.

For once, I was in control, and got the best sex I've had with her for a long while. She was sulky this morning, but I'm used to that. She'll make me suffer for a while, with her moods, and sex will be off the agenda for a couple of weeks. But then we'll get back to normal, whatever that means these days.

The family gathering was dull enough, but at least her mother was talking to me, so that's one problem out of the way. Later on, I was playing cards with Ben and Frank in a room at the back of the sprawling house. The cousin was there too, the bastard who'd come to my house with them.

It all seemed to be relaxed enough, but then after a hand, Ben looked across at me. "So what did you do to her?"

"What do you mean?"

"She's let something slip out, about you forcing yourself on her last night."

I felt sick. I never expected her to talk about it. And what woman tells her brother about her sex life?

"It wasn't like that. But what we do in our bedroom is private, and it's not something to discuss."

"It's not private, because she told me. And there's a lot to discuss. Why did you do it?"

He wasn't going to let the matter drop. April must have told him every detail.

"Listen, Ben, put yourself in my position. We were ready to have sex, and I was all worked up, and getting started. You're a man, so you know how it is. Then she changed her mind. But it was too late, and I couldn't help carrying on. That's all it was."

Ben picked up the pack, and shuffled it.

"So you raped my little sister."

"No, I told you what happened. It's not rape. It was a misunderstanding between us. Hell, it happens with all couples."

Ben looked at the others. "Let's go, then."

The two of them stood up, and came behind me.

Then my chair was pulled backwards, and they dragged me down to the floor. I struggled, but with two of them, I wasn't strong enough. "Stop it, Ben. I've explained it, haven't I?"

Ben opened a door, and they pulled me towards it. Shit, it was a cellar. The last place I wanted to be. I tried to get away, but they were too much for me, and I was dragged down the stone steps.

At the bottom, they lifted me to stand upright, and Ben stood in front of me. "You're due for another lesson. Do I need to gag you again?"

"No, don't do that, please."

Ben nodded to the others. They pulled me round, and laid me face down across the width of a table, with my head over one side, and legs hanging down on the other side. Then they spread my arms apart, and ran a rope from one wrist to the other, passing under the table. I couldn't move, and with the tension in my arms, it wasn't easy to breathe.

Ben said, "Get his pants off."

They fumbled around to undo them, then I felt them taken off, and then my briefs.

I remembered the last time with this crowd, and how Ben beat me with the poker. I hoped to God they wouldn't do worse.

Ben came and stood next to me. "You've a nice leather belt on your pants. Let's see what I can do with it."

He moved from view, and I waited.

Then a faint noise before it struck. The pain was as sharp as a sting, all across my buttocks. It subsided a little, then he hit me again, and again, until I lost count. I wanted to shout out, but I couldn't stand the thought of that gag. All I could feel in my buttocks was pain and numbness.

Ben came round to me again. "Now you're going to see how it feels to be raped."

I feared what was coming. Maybe something like that poker. "Please don't do that to me. I won't be any trouble again."

Ben laughed. "I'm not going to do anything. Frank's going to do it."

There was a shuffling noise. I could guess he'd be taking off his pants.

I said, "Ben, please don't."

"Is that what sis said when you were raping her?"

I wanted to reason with him, but it was too late. I felt something hard pushing against my anus, and hurting like hell.

Then Frank said, "I can't do it. He's too tight."

The cousin laughed, "Maybe your dick's too big for him. Put some grease on it."

A minute later, Frank was back. I felt him again behind me. It was hurting more every time he pushed. But I wrenched my face to keep quiet.

Then suddenly he was into me. It was still painful, but less so, and almost a relief.

Almost immediately he ejaculated, with a sigh of satisfaction.

Frank's a man of simple pleasures. He withdrew, and my anus relaxed. It was sore, but I was glad it was over.

Frank said to the cousin. "That was good. Like fucking a virgin. Why don't you have a go?"

I dreaded the response.

Then he said, "No, I don't think so."

I relaxed. Maybe it was over.

He walked round in front of me. "I've got a better idea."

He unzipped his pants, and pulled out his penis, and pressed it into my face. The smell of stale urine was revolting. This guy probably never washed.

He said, "Suck it, you stupid fucker."

I lifted my head, but hesitated.

Then I heard Ben's voice behind me. "Being awkward, are you? Maybe this'll motivate you. I'll keep doing this until he tells me to stop."

Then a blow across the buttocks again from that belt. It brought back the pain across the whole area. What else could I do? I opened my mouth and let his penis in, then closed my lips around it as it hardened.

Another blow across my buttocks.

I started sucking. Hard as I could.

He said, "Okay Ben, you can hold off. He's doing me now."

I carried on, with it getting firmer as I sucked. I dreaded what was coming, but it was inevitable, and I wanted it finished.

Then he ejaculated. It was horrible, and I had to swallow, but I kept my mouth round him, until he decided to withdraw. I couldn't risk that belt again.

They stood around laughing as he zipped up, and Frank put his pants back on.

Ben undid the wrist restraints.

"Get dressed and back up there. And listen, if I have to deal with you again, I don't care what April says. I'll take you somewhere quiet, and I'll kill you. And I'll make it worse than you can imagine. I'll start by cutting your balls off, and letting you cry for a while. You'll take a long time to die."

# Part 6 – SWAPPING HUSBANDS

# 29

*~ ~ ~ ~ April ~ ~ ~ ~*

Robin was out, so it was a relief to get with Dawn this evening, and leave Grant to mope around.

Dawn said, "Is Grant still sulking? It's been a week now hasn't it?"

"Oh he's still having long silences, and we haven't talked much, other than what we have to. I've gone to bed early a couple of times, to get away from him."

"They must have beaten him up terribly. He's taken it much worse than last time, hasn't he?"

"It was pretty awful what they did, but he deserved it after forcing himself on me."

"What did Ben actually do?"

"It wasn't very pleasant. I told Ben to teach him a lesson again, and to make sure he suffered, but Ben does tend to go to extremes."

"So, tell me, what did he do?"

"All right, but don't tell Robin. They tied him up, and took off his pants. And then he got a whipping from Ben. And, are you sure you want to know everything?"

She nodded, eyes open wide.

"And then Frank sodomized him."

"Good Lord, no wonder he's sulking. If Frank had humped me, I'd probably feel the same. It must have been horrible for him."

"I don't care. He deserved it. I thought he'd been getting better, although he had been awkward with me at times, but then when he … Well, he got justice. Now he'll behave, you'll see."

Dawn frowned. "Will he, though? It's Ben he's scared of, not you. And however bad it was, the memory will fade with time. He'll need reminding, or he'll drift back again."

"I'll have to think about that. But I see what you mean. Grant has to respect me for myself, not because I can call on Ben. But I still want him as my husband and lover, so it's all very difficult. And the mood he's in, who knows how long that's going to last."

"Maybe you both need to go away together for a break. Somewhere to take your mind off all this? Robin and I could come with you if you want."

"That's a brilliant idea. Grant and I both have leave due, so we can go anytime. But where would we go?"

Dawn looked thoughtful. "I haven't been to Las Vegas for years. What do you think?"

"A week in Vegas would be marvelous. And I might try roulette. I always wanted to, but I only played the slots when I went before."

Dawn laughed. "What I remember most about the place was the young men from Hicksville looking for new experiences, with booze, smoking and women. They were all desperate to get laid before they went back home. You and I'd be better going without the men."

"Maybe, but what I want is to get Grant to move on, so we do need to take them along. But now you've got me thinking, and I've an idea for some fun with them. And I know that you'll approve."

# 30

It was evening, and I was watching TV, when she came in and switched it off.

"Grant, darling. What you did was disgraceful, and you've been punished for it. But we've got to get on with our lives. Are you ready to do that?"

I nodded, and mumbled, "I guess so."

"Then come on. Let's go to my bedroom."

That woke me up. "Does that mean …?"

She screwed her face up as if she was deciding. "I'll tell you what. There's a little game I want to play with you, and then you can make love to me, for as long as you want."

In the bedroom, as we undressed, I didn't care what the game was. She was getting her way again, but I didn't mind.

I headed for the bed, but she blocked my way. She'd got two sets of handcuffs in her hand. "If you're ready for my game, sit on the edge of the bed."

I sat down, and she handcuffed my wrists, and then my ankles.

I said, "What sort of game is it?"

"I'm going to be a dominatrix and you're going to be my submissive."

"I told you before, you're not the type."

She got out some clothing from the cupboard, and started dressing in front of me. A black corset, black stockings, and high heels. The corset covered her breasts, but with an opening for each nipple. Then finally a wig, with long black hair. Incredibly sexy.

I said, "Can't we skip the game? I'm ready for you now."

"Patience, darling."

111

She applied her lipstick and checked herself in the mirror.

Then she came over to where I was sitting, with what looked like a riding whip. Her lipstick was black too. She looked kind of Gothic.

"Don't you see me as a dominatrix now?"

"You look the part, no question. But that doesn't make you one."

She frowned, then went back to look at herself in the mirror, and flicked the whip. Then back to me.

"What you need to understand is that now I'm dressed for it, I'm not pretending. Like an actress who's got into the part, and forgotten who she really is. I'm your dominatrix now, so you can forget about April. And I'm going to make you submit to me."

She flicked the whip at my body, and it stung.

"Hey, April, that hurt."

"Don't call me that. If you speak to me, you have to address me as 'mistress'."

She fondled the whip, then flicked it again at me.

"Hey, it hurt."

This time, she swung it hard on me, and the pain was sudden and sharp. "Don't say anything unless you call me 'mistress'."

"Well, it hurt, mistress."

She leaned down and kissed me with her black lips. "That's better. Now get on your knees."

"Do I have to?"

The whip slashed into me. I jumped to my feet. "That's enough."

She struck me again. "Say mistress!"

I tried to move forward towards her, but she was quick, and with my feet tied, I crashed over to the floor. She stood over me. "Tell me you're sorry."

I couldn't get up easily without her hitting me with that whip again.

"I'm sorry, mistress."

"Good. Now on hands and knees."

When I got into position, she came behind me. "You've still got marks from what they did to you."

"I know that, mistress."

She sat on me, legs astride. "Don't make me have to whip you now, as I may decide to whip your buttocks too. Now move around slowly, like a horse I'm riding."

I felt stupid, and it wasn't easy with my wrists and ankles tied, but I wasn't going to argue. I was dreading her hitting my behind.

She got off me. "I want you to carry on around the room. And every now and then you've to say you want to be my submissive."

So I started.

She sat on the bed and watched me while I moved around, and chanted my words, until my knees were feeling sore.

Then she went and stood by the mirror, looking at herself.

She called to me. "You can stop now. Come over here, and kneel so you can see yourself in the mirror."

She wandered off and then was back. With some black thing with leather straps.

As she put it on, I realized it was a dildo.

When she'd tightened the straps, she looked in the mirror, and swiveled round to see it from different angles.

She laughed. "It must be funny having one of these all the time."

Then she looked down at me, kneeling next to her.

"Now tell me you want to suck my penis."

"No, I won't, that's going too far."

She swung her arm, and I braced myself. I wasn't going to admit weakness to her. So I kept silent when the whip made contact, even though I wanted to shout out. This time, I knew she'd drawn blood.

She paused, then, "Tell me you want to suck it."

I kept quiet.

"Right," she said. "Now I'll show you what a dominatrix does when her submissive doesn't behave."

She struck me again on my back. Then again, and she kept on hitting me, every few seconds, over and over. The pain was getting worse, and there was nothing I could do to escape.

I shouted out, "Please, mistress, stop!"

But she carried on. Part of my back felt cold, and I knew it was bleeding. But I couldn't get up to stop her, and if I rolled on my back, she might do worse. She was out of control.

I kept begging, "Please, mistress, …"

Until finally she stopped.

She said, "Now tell me."

There were tears in my eyes, and I could hardly get the words out. "I want to suck your penis, mistress."

"All right then, do it."

She looked down on me, without emotion, as if I was a child finally doing what I was told.

I put my lips round it, and sucked. It tasted of rubber.

She said, "That's better."

She put her hands on the sides of my head, and pulled me towards her, so the dildo went further into my mouth. The taste nearly made me sick.

Then she said, "Now back and forth. Pretend you're enjoying it."

I moved my head as she said. I could see myself in the mirror, looking like a homosexual giving a blow job. But I made it as realistic as I could. She was stroking the whip on my back.

Then, "All right, that's enough."

I pulled away, then she unstrapped the thing and dropped it.

She pulled me over to lie flat on my back on the floor, and stood over me.

"So let me ask you again. Do you think I make a good dominatrix?"

She was still holding the whip.

"Yes, mistress."

"Then the game's over. And you get your reward now."

She undressed, and then released the cuffs.

I stood up, and grabbed hold of her. "You shouldn't have done that, you've hurt my back."

She's usually so angelic, but her face contorted. "You'll do what I say from now on, and you'll never tell me off. If you ever make me angry again, I'll really hurt you. And don't think I can't, now you know what I'm capable of."

It was scary, seeing her switch on a different, almost vicious, personality.

I sat on the bed. "Okay, okay."

She was still scowling, "I'm in control here, not you. So you'll obey me, and get used to it. And if you've any doubts what I can do, remember that I can easily wait until you're asleep, or even drug you. So tell me, who is in control?"

I stuttered, "You are."

Then she brightened. She went over to the mirror, and wiped off the black lipstick. Then she came back to me and kissed me.

"Now darling, make love to me."

# 31

I found out that I'd got the job, late on Friday, and I was so excited over the weekend. I'd told Grant and Dawn, but more than anything I wanted to see the reaction of my colleagues. Especially the ones who I beat to the job.

I got in early this morning to move my personal stuff before everyone else arrived, and most importantly, I moved my nameplate. It's a corner office now, with windows on two sides. I think I'll have some plants grow there.

It's funny, but during the day I already noticed that people were treating me differently. A lot more people wanted to say hello. But I have to behave differently too, to match my new position. It's not that I don't want to be friendly with the people lower down, but they're hardly the ones I need to cultivate.

In the evening, I had my first invite to a senior staff dinner, at a conference center downtown.

Grant had driven me there. "What time do you want me back here?"

"I wasn't expecting you to go away."

"Hey, I have to eat too."

"Well go somewhere local then, and come straight back. I don't know when it'll be finished."

"But you could be hours."

"I don't think so. It's a working meal, with managers giving presentations while we eat. When it's over, everyone will want to leave."

It was what I'd expected. A buffet-style meal, so it was easy to circulate between the courses and the talks.

I finally cornered my VP. "Hi, have you a speech to give too?"

He laughed. "A small one, a thank you at the end. Are you enjoying it?"

"It's been great. And a good way to meet the other executives away from the office."

"I hear there have been some threats against you. Is it something we should worry about?"

"No. It's someone I laid off. The stupid man's been making a fuss, when he should have been getting himself a job. He blames me and a couple of others for the mess he's in, when really it's himself that's to blame. It'll blow over soon enough."

"Well, let me know if there's anything we can do. You're becoming a key member of the team, and we need to look after you."

I smiled. "I'm not sure the company worries about such things."

"Maybe not, but I do."

I fluttered my false eyelashes, hoping it wasn't too obvious.

"I value that. Very much."

For a moment he was lost for words. Then, "By the way, what's happening about your old job?"

"I'll have to get with human resources and sort out the selection criteria and all that. It'll take a while, but I've put a young man in as acting manager, meantime. Name of Scott."

"Is he good enough to do the job permanently?"

"I'm sure of it. But we have to follow procedure."

"All right. Now come over here with me, and I'll introduce you to the president of the company."

It was later than I expected by the time I was out of there, and Grant seemed to be grumpy as we drove home.

"I'm sorry, Grant. If I'd known it was going on that late, I wouldn't have had you wait. But there was a lot of networking and discussion afterwards, and I could hardly walk out on the president of the company."

"Well, I am annoyed, but there's something else. Your VP's chauffeur was there with his limo, so I got talking to him. Even had a couple of beers from the drinks cupboard in the car. He said that they all knew about the threats to the company from that guy you got rid of, and that you were one of the people he'd been complaining about."

"I told you it's nothing. The chauffeur's repeating gossip. In fact I was talking about it with the VP, and no one is taking it as a serious threat to me or anyone else. The man's a loser, sounding off."

"Are you sure? Maybe I should pay him a visit?"

# 32

I've not got anything against Scott. He's a nice enough guy. But I wasn't sure about having him round the house. He moved in two nights ago, to sleep in the spare room, without much notice. But he should be gone soon.

April was working late again, so it was a chance to talk to him.

"It's good of you to let me stay, Grant. It saves a lot of hassle."

"Is your new place nearly ready?"

"They're finishing off the painting. Then a day to dry, and the furniture goes in. It's a dump, and I'll have to get something better, but it's all I could find to rent at short notice."

"April says you left your girlfriend and that's what's caused the trouble."

Scott smiled. "I told her I was leaving, and next thing her father's there, shouting his head off, and moving my belongings out. I thought I'd be on the sofa a few days, but suddenly I was homeless. I should have got everything ready, and walked out."

"What happened with her? An argument that went too far?"

"No, not really. I'd got tired of the situation. Anyway, April says I'll be better off without her. She'd be no good for my career. And April's usually right."

"And you're doing April's old job now?"

"Yes, and that's caused some friction. But I don't care. It's a good experience move, for my resume, even if I don't get it permanently. And it's nothing to the hassle April got

119

with her move upwards. There's a lot of jealousy in that place."

"You get on well with April, don't you?"

"I guess so."

His face went a slight pink. Guilty. But what the hell. I knew he'd been to her bedroom last night. And it was over two hours before he went back to his room. So it was a lot more than a goodnight kiss.

I thought of challenging him about it. But why embarrass him? He probably had as much choice as I do with her, given that she's his boss.

"Well, we're away from work next week, and off to Las Vegas."

"So I heard. You'll have fun there, everyone does. And there's that old phrase, 'What happens in Vegas stays in Vegas'. If you get away from April, I know a great bar. Topless girls, and the beer's only —"

I laughed. "Don't worry. April says she has plans. If they include a bar, then I'll be in a bar, otherwise, forget it."

# 33

We'd booked this vacation at short notice, and I wasn't hopeful about what would be available, but we got a great ground-floor suite, right near the pool. There were two bedrooms, each with a double bed. The beds are only regular-size, so Grant grumbled about it, but it doesn't bother the rest of us.

We'd all slept well that first night, and then after breakfast, Dawn and I went for a stroll, while the men sunbathed. On the way back, we found a shady spot to sit, looking across at the men lying stretched out. Robin looked pale and skinny against Grant, but he still looked pretty good compared with most of the other men nearby, with their rolls of flab and hairy bodies.

That's when I suggested swapping.

Dawn had hinted at it often enough in the past, and I'd laughed it off, but now she could see I was serious. It was what I'd planned, and I thought she'd jump at the opportunity, but she didn't answer straight away.

"Dawn, maybe I've spoken out of turn. We're on vacation. Maybe we should settle for that?"

She smiled now. "But that's what makes it perfect. If we do swap, and we regret it, we can put it down to being on vacation. And people do all sorts of crazy things on vacation. Especially here."

"So you admit it's crazy."

"A little. But what's wrong with that, if it's fun?"

"I don't know if I'm comfortable about Grant sleeping with someone else, even you. How do you feel about Robin?"

121

"It will be good for them. And they won't say no, not that we'd let them. You'll like Robin. He's very sensuous. Very gentle."

I laughed, "And I'm sure you'll like Grant. I couldn't say he was sensuous. Once he gets going, he can be a wild beast. And since he went on the steroids, he seems stronger than ever."

"It sounds exciting. So let's do it tonight."

"Tonight? Now I'm getting nervous. Are you sure?"

"Why not? Are you scared of what Grant might say? That he'll refuse to do it?"

"Grant will do what I tell him."

Dawn smiled. "We'll have to watch their reactions. They'll love the idea, but they'll be careful not to show it."

~ ~ ~ ~ *Grant* ~ ~ ~ ~

The vacation was a great idea. We all had a pleasant day around the hotel and by the pool. The girls went off for walks, and Robin and I sunbathed and drank beer. I've decided that Robin's okay. I wasn't too sure before, as he's nothing like my other friends, but we get on well together.

In the evening we ate out, then when we got back, April made her announcement.

She clapped her hands for us to stop talking. "Now listen. I've something important to say."

She smiled and looked at me. "Dawn and I have decided we want to try something for a change tonight. We're swapping husbands. Now what do you think of that?"

I looked across at Robin, but he was showing nothing. Maybe he already knew. Then at Dawn. She was smiling at me. There was nothing I'd want more than to sleep with her. But not with April around. And did April really want to sleep with Robin?

I said, "April, can we have a private word?"

In the bedroom, I said, "What brought this on? Aren't I enough for you?"

"Of course you are. But Dawn and I were talking about you and Robin, and well, I said you were very assertive when we had sex, and she said Robin was the opposite. Anyway, I don't know how we got round to it, but Dawn suggested we swap for the night. I thought you'd be pleased. I know you like her."

I could feel my face flush.

"That's not the point. Don't you mind me having sex with your sister?"

"I won't be there, so it won't matter to me. Anyway you'll only have sex if she wants it."

"And will you be having sex with Robin?"

She looked thoughtful. "I don't know. I've known him so long, it'll be weird to share a bed with him. So I don't think I will have sex. But it all depends what mood I'm in."

"What about his mood?"

"Don't be silly. Men are always in the mood. Even Robin."

Back in the living room, I had another drink. I needed it.

It had all happened so fast, that I didn't have time to think. I couldn't believe the cool way April announced it. And they gave us no chance to argue. Not that Robin said anything anyway.

And now Dawn was watching me, the tethered goat. She stood up and faced me.

"Come on then, Grant."

As soon as the bedroom door closed, she put her arms round me, and looked up into my eyes.

"Kiss me, Grant."

Her lips pouted ready for me.

I embraced her too, and kissed her, feeling her tongue straight away on my lips. It was a long kiss, and passionate.

When we came apart, she said, "I've always had a crush on you. Right from when we all first met. We'll have some fun tonight, won't we?"

"Aren't you bothered that Robin's sleeping with April?"

123

"Not at all. Now you can start by undressing me. And do it slowly."

I started taking her clothes off, and she started on mine. All very slowly, step by step. She told me to slow down a couple of times. By the time we were naked, I had an erection.

She took hold of it, as if feeling a vegetable in a shop. "My God, it's massive."

"You've no inhibitions, have you, Dawn?"

She smiled and got onto the bed, lying on her back, with her hands behind her head.

I went to stand at the foot of the bed, looking down on her. Not as delicate as April, but curvaceous and very sexy.

She smiled. "You can fuck me now, Grant. As hard as you like."

~ ~ ~ ~ *April* ~ ~ ~ ~

I'd always wondered what Dawn saw in Robin. But I was getting the idea. He's different from Grant, but that doesn't make him any less a person.

I don't think he was concerned about having sex at all, and only wanted to cuddle me. But I knew what Dawn would be doing, and I wasn't going to be short-changed.

Once I got him going, Robin was actually very good. He wanted a lot more foreplay than Grant, and it went on for ages, and was almost dreamlike. I would have been happy to fall asleep with him doing that, but I had to get my full share. So I told him I'd had enough, and it was time for him to make love to me.

He was surprisingly agile, and so good at keeping himself up above me, that he hardly pressed down at all, while he made love to me. Such a change from Grant. And different again from Scott.

As I lay there afterwards, I could imagine myself having Robin as a husband, and sleeping with him every night. He wasn't the sort of man I'd have looked for, but I would have been happy with him. I cuddled up to him, and kissed him.

I slept well that night.

Next morning, Robin was up early preparing breakfast, and Grant was in the bathroom, so Dawn and I went for a walk round the pool.

Dawn asked, "So was Robin any good last night?"

"Yes, he was. I'll be happy to be back with Grant, but it was an interesting experience."

"No feelings of guilt then?

"You know, Dawn, I hadn't even thought about it. I enjoyed sleeping with Robin, but it doesn't seem to matter that he's really yours. And it doesn't mean I love Grant any less."

"So you're glad we did it?"

"Yes. Robin is so different, so caring. And I'd do it again sometime, if you want that."

"Well, not for a while. Your beast was insatiable, and he wore me out. I'll settle for going back to Robin."

"They don't know what we want to do tonight, do they?"

Dawn smiled. "Then let's have a bit of fun with them."

Grant looked tired when we sat down for breakfast. Whatever Dawn had said, it looked to me as though it was her that had worn him out, rather than the other way round.

Now it was Dawn's turn to tell them.

"Listen you two. April and I have decided to keep with the swap for the day. When we go out, I'll be with Grant, and April with Robin. We'll hold hands, and kiss, and behave like we're newlyweds. Don't you think that'll be fun?"

Grant looked at Robin, and asked, "And tonight?"

Dawn said, "We haven't decided yet."

During the day, we visited casinos, and some shops, and did touristy things. We split up more than once, and in some ways I preferred being with Robin. He knows a lot more about art and history than Grant, and he's always a gentleman, without being told. Dawn seemed to enjoy being with Grant too, parading him around the same way that I do.

In the evening, at dinner, Dawn finally told them that we were back with our own partners. Robin and Grant nodded, revealing nothing, but I'd have loved to know what they were thinking.


~ ~ ~ ~ *Grant* ~ ~ ~ ~

It was a relief to be back in the bedroom with April.

I like Dawn, and it was great sex last night, but spending all day with her was getting me down. She's even more domineering than April, and constantly telling me I ought to learn more. As if I cared about some old painting or whatever.

Not that it was all bad. We split off from the others for a while, and then Dawn really got into the young-lovers theme. She wouldn't let go of my hand, and every now and then she'd pull me towards her for a kiss, usually when someone was coming along. She's an exhibitionist, and I was what she wanted for her performance.

When we were in bed with the lights out, April said, "Dawn told me you were really good last night."

"So you've been talking about it?"

"That's half the fun. She said that you were a bit rough, but I think she liked that too. I'm sure that she'd swap permanently if she got the chance. But I'm not having that."

"What about you?"

"Robin's nice, and I could sleep with him again sometime, but I wouldn't want to make it permanent."

She talked so matter of fact about it all, as if it was nothing unusual.

"April, you keep surprising me. I never expected any of this when we got married."

126

"It's Dawn's fault. She kept on and on, so in the end it was easiest to go along with it. It's been fun for you though hasn't it?"

It was true. "I suppose so. But I'm glad to be back with you."

"Same here. Robin takes it nice and slow in bed. And he really is gentle. But it wasn't as good as when we have it."

We lay there for a while. Then April said, "I'm in the mood, if you are."

I laughed. "I might be."

"Then you're not still exhausted from last night?"

"No, I've got over that. I'm in good shape."

"Then I want the kind of sex you gave my sister. Whatever what you did with her, I want exactly the same."

# 34

It was the last day of the vacation, so we all had a final dinner out, with lots to drink, before heading back to the hotel.

Earlier in the day, Dawn had been on at me to swap again for our last night, but I refused. I wouldn't have minded sharing a bed with Robin, but I wasn't interested in having sex with him again so soon. And I knew that she would be doing things all night long with Grant if she could. It wasn't a fair swap. Finally she accepted it, and dropped the subject, but she wasn't happy.

It was later in the afternoon, when she broached another idea. I thought at first she was joking, but she was deadly serious. And it seemed clever on two counts. Dawn and me together, but also seeing how the men reacted.

Back at the hotel, and after a couple more drinks, Dawn said, "So boys, what sleeping arrangements would you prefer tonight?"

They looked at each other, knowing that there was no safe answer.

Grant said, "I don't mind. Whatever you choose."

Robin nodded agreement.

Dawn said, "Well, you like experimenting, don't you? So there's no point in my sleeping with Robin, and April with Grant. I wonder what we could do then?"

The boys stayed silent.

Dawn continued, "And we already had a night for me with Grant, and April with Robin, so that would be a bit boring too. So there was only one thing we could think of."

I looked at them. "Tonight I'm going to be sleeping with Dawn. We used to share a bed when we were girls, and it'll be fun, like then."

Grant said, "What about us?"

I replied, "You boys can share the other bed. You can have fun together too, if you want."

Grant muttered, "Don't be stupid."

"I'm not being stupid. I've tried Robin out, and he can be really nice and gentle in bed."

Dawn added, "Robin, don't listen to her. I'd leave Grant alone. Once he gets going he's a real beast, and you won't be able to stop him."

I couldn't help giggling, and then Dawn burst out laughing.

The men weren't amused.


~ ~ ~ ~ *Grant* ~ ~ ~ ~


In bed with Robin, I was tense. The bed wasn't that large, and it was difficult keeping apart.

April and Dawn had treated it as a great joke. No doubt they were in bed now, and laughing about it.

The problem with the air-conditioning was the last straw. The room was hot, even with the window ajar, and we couldn't have more than a single sheet over us without getting too warm. It was too hot for nightwear, but I kept my briefs on. Robin was naked next to me.

What made it worse was April giving me a good night kiss before we went to bed, and asking me to be nice to Robin. As if we were homosexuals.

It was the middle of the night when I woke. The air was cool, so at least the air con was running again.

For a moment I thought I was with April, until the truth dawned on me.

I was lying against his back, and I had my arm around him.

129

His body small compared to mine, and his skin so soft, I could have been holding a woman.

I had to get out of this, but without waking him.

Then I really got into trouble. I was getting an erection, and it had slipped out from my briefs, and was touching him.

I slowly withdrew my arm, and then turned over to face away from him. I was as careful as I could, not to disturb him. But as I listened in the dark, his breathing wasn't steady.

I had a feeling he was awake.


~ ~ ~ ~ *April* ~ ~ ~ ~


It was hot, so Dawn and I were naked, lying on top of the bed. It was strange being in the same bed, after so many years.

Dawn cuddled up to me. "It's nice being together, isn't it?"

"Like when we were young girls."

"I wonder what the boys are doing in there? Do you think anything's going on?"

"No, Grant's not into that. He's not keen on homosexuals."

"He looked in the mood for something, earlier on."

"That's probably because he thought he'd be with you. And that blouse you were wearing, with no bra … No wonder he was in the mood."

Dawn was quiet for a while, then, "Do you think I've got nice breasts?"

"They're perfect. And so firm, you don't need a bra, except for covering up."

Dawn took hold of my hand, and put it on her breast. Her nipple was huge.

She said, "It's a lovely feeling with your hand on me. It's so small and delicate."

130

Then her hand came onto my breast. "Does that feel good too?"

I was excited at what she was doing, but … "Stop it, Dawn."

She didn't take it away, but started moving her fingertips on my nipple. I could feel it getting harder.

"Dawn, you shouldn't."

"But doesn't it feel natural? After all we are sisters, and we've shared a bed before. I used to play with you then, so why not now? We're here in Vegas, and we can do what we want."

I moved my fingers over her breast, up against the nipple, as she'd done with me, and very gently stroked it.

She was right. It was natural. And my fingertips slid so easily across her smooth skin.

After a few minutes, Dawn moved up over me, and knelt looking down.

Then she kissed me. We've kissed many times, but rarely on the lips since we were girls. I responded. My hand had come away from her breast, but she was still stroking mine. Then she moved her head down and kissed my nipples.

She whispered, "Guess what I'm going to do next."

I'd been holding my breath. "I don't know."

"My little sister, my darling. I'm going to make love to you."

# Part 7 – A STALKER IS MURDERED

## 35

~ ~ ~ ~ *Grant* ~ ~ ~ ~

April's mother opened the door and looked me up and down as if to verify it was really me, then she waved me in. It was my first time at her house, aside from those awful family get-togethers.

She'd called April, who'd sent me off straight away. I was told to take all my tools, but no idea why. I wasn't enthusiastic about seeing her, but at least it seemed to be for some purpose.

"Grant. It's a problem with the air conditioner. It's been vibrating, and no one seems to be able to fix it. I'll show you."

I followed her down into the basement. It was creepy thinking of the last time I'd been down here. The air con looked old, but solid enough. And she was right: there was a vibration somewhere. You could hear it, and with a hand on the unit, you could feel it.

She said, "The engineer told me that the whole system's worn out and needs replacing. I said that was nonsense, and it should last a lot longer than that. I paid a lot of money for it."

I felt sorry for the engineer. No doubt she said a lot more than that.

"I'll have a look, but I don't know much about this type of equipment. It's probably the fan or the bearings, and they might be sealed up. And if you've had an engineer out already —"

"I've had two of them. And had to pay. All for nothing. The problem's still there. Ben had a look at it too, but he's got nowhere. Mind you, he's not an engineer like you. Anyway, I'll leave you to it."

So off she went upstairs. No offer of a coffee. Not that I was expecting it.

I unscrewed the side panels. I hadn't been sure what I'd be able to do, and getting the panels off didn't help. Behind them, most of it was riveted or welded. The blower was running full speed, and that was probably where the problem lay. Close to the blower casing, I could hear the noise. But standing back from the unit, the noise didn't seem any louder with the panels off, which was odd.

I grabbed hold of the whole assembly, and pulled at it. The noise of the blower carried on, but the vibration stopped. The wall mountings must have come loose over time. So, it was the whole damned unit that had been vibrating on the wall. I tightened the bolts as hard as I could, and pulled at the unit to be sure. Then back on with the panels. Problem solved.

I took my tools upstairs, and called out. She appeared from the kitchen.

I said, "I don't know if it's a permanent fix, but it's a lot better than it was."

She frowned, and proceeded down the stairs, with me following. It was like waiting for the teacher to inspect my work.

She stood there and listened. "You're right. It's quiet now. Thank goodness for that." She turned to me. "Well done."

Those words were worth a lot to me. It was the first time we'd had any sort of normal conversation, and now she was actually complimenting me. And smiling, looking quite attractive. I hadn't really noticed before, as at those family gatherings she was always so serious and aloof. But in casual clothes, and a cheerful mood, I could see where April and Dawn's looks came from. I'm not one for older women, not normally anyway, but if I was still single, and had met her somewhere, I'd probably have made a pass.

As I left the house, she was still smiling, and so was I.


When I got home, I put my tools away, then went into the living room, where April was sitting.

I should have guessed something was up, as she'd normally be reading or watching TV. But she was sitting there, looking into space.

She looked up. "Were you able to help?"

"I sure was. It was a problem with her air con, and I fixed it."

I laughed. "It's unbelievable. I think I'm finally becoming accepted, because I fixed her air con."

She smiled. But she looked preoccupied.

I said, "What's up? Is there a problem?"

"While you were out, I had a phone call from the police. It's about that man I fired, the one that was making threats."

"Have they arrested him?"

"No. The thing is, he's been found dead. He's been murdered."

"Jesus! Do they know who did it?"

"No, I don't think so."

"At least he won't bother you any more. I'm sorry to hear of anyone being murdered, but in his case —"

She interrupted, "Grant, the police want to talk to me. You too."

# 36

There were two of them, neither in uniform. Detectives. Grant showed them in, and then came and sat next to me.

The senior detective was a big fellow, with a middle-aged spread, and a weary face. The other one was younger, and hovered in the background.

The senior one said, "Did you know anything about the murder before I called you?"

I replied, "Nothing. It was a surprise, a shock even. We've been away, and we'd heard nothing. To be honest, officer, I can't feel too emotional about it. He was an unpleasant man."

"That's as may be, but can you explain your involvement with him?"

"I was his manager, and I have to admit we had our differences. He was sloppy about company practices, and thought that was acceptable behavior. I had more than one argument with him about that."

"And that's why you fired him?"

"No, it wasn't like that. The company had a round of downsizing, and he was one of the unlucky ones. As his manager, I was the one who told him he would have to go. It's never a nice thing, and there was another employee affected too. But that's business. And since then I've not seen him or talked to him."

"But you've heard from him?"

"Only indirectly. He'd tried phoning for me at the office a couple of times, but I wouldn't take the calls."

"Any reason why not?"

135

"There was nothing to gain from it. It wouldn't have been productive for me or the company. I'd heard he was still bitter about losing his job, and I had no wish to hear him moaning about it."

The detective looked at his notes. "I understand there were threats towards you?"

"Me and others. But don't you have threats against you too?"

He nodded. "I sure do. It goes with the job."

"And do you take them seriously?"

"No, not usually."

"Well, that's my attitude too. I knew that he'd eventually get a job, and move on, but meantime he'd be saying all sorts of silly things."

The detective glanced at his young colleague, who shrugged.

"I think that's all for now, then. But I need to verify your whereabouts last week. It's —"

Grant interrupted, "Why? You surely don't think of my wife as a suspect?"

The detective laughed. "No, not at all." He turned to me. "You don't exactly have the physique to beat a man to death."

Then he turned to Grant, and his eyes hardened. It was obvious what he was thinking.

"At this stage, we have no obvious motive, so we have to keep everyone on our list as potential suspects, and go through a process of elimination. And I'm afraid that includes both of you. We need to know your general movements last week, and in particular where you both were the night before last."

Grant said, "Well, we were in Las Vegas all week, so that should eliminate us. We only came back yesterday."

"Fine. Let this officer have the details of your flights, and where you were staying."

After they'd gone, Grant said, "It's lucky we were in Vegas, wasn't it? We wouldn't have had much of an alibi if we'd been here."

"I suppose not, as it happened at night."

Grant looked thoughtful. "I know it's awful to say so, but I'm not unhappy that he's dead. You might not have taken the threats seriously, but I was worried for you."

I didn't tell Grant that I'd been worried too, especially when I'd seen the man hanging around the office building. I'd told Dawn, and Ben, so maybe I should have told Grant.

But it didn't matter any more, now the problem had gone away.

# 37

It was our first meal together since the Vegas trip. April and Dawn looking fabulous, and Robin and me doing our best. We make a good foursome.

Robin said, "Vegas gets better all the time. You could go every year and get a different experience."

Dawn smiled. "If you ask me which experience was best, the swapping gets my vote. It was a great little vacation."

April said, "So, would you go again next year?"

"Yes, but maybe we'll leave the boys behind next time."

April blushed slightly, but was saved by Robin breaking in, "Don't forget, we had fun too. Don't leave us out of the plans, April."

"Oh, you liked all the swapping around, did you? With me? Or was it better with Grant?"

Robin was the one to blush now. It was time to change the subject.

I said, "Vegas was great. But on another matter, how did your interview with the police go?"

Dawn leaned forward confidentially, "It was quite exciting. You two are on their list of suspects, and they asked us all sorts of questions about where you were at various times. I didn't say who was sleeping with whom, but you've got your alibis okay."

April said, "So now we're off the list, did they indicate what they're doing next?"

"The old guy didn't tell me anything, but he got called away, and the young one opened up, even more so after Robin left the room. I'm sure I asked him more questions

138

than he asked me. There are a couple more people where you work, and there were issues in his personal life too. He seems to have made quite a few enemies. But so far, the police haven't anything positive, so there's no prospect of an arrest."

I said, "I'm surprised he told you all that. But that means the investigation is going nowhere?"

"That's right. They're being pressured to close the case. But did you hear how he got killed?"

April said, "I don't want to know."

I leaned forward, "I do."

Robin added, "Me too. It was a beating wasn't it?"

"That's right. It was about three in the morning. An intruder broke in at the back of the house, and went to his bedroom, and battered him to death in his bed. The pathologist says it was probably an aluminum baseball bat that was used. The poor guy never even woke up. Killed by the first blow, but then his face was beaten over and over after he died."

I said, "It sounds like a hate crime."

"That's what the detectives think. There was cash stolen, but they don't think that was the motive. It was too savage. A maniac rather than a thief. There's a chance that forensics will throw up some clue, but they're not hopeful. So whoever did it is probably going to get away with it."

Robin said, "That happens too often, and it's not right."

Dawn shook her head. "I don't agree. The guy was a menace, and whoever did it, I'm glad he did."

April added, "I agree with Dawn. I don't mind if they never catch him."

# 38

The atmosphere at the family gathering was relaxed. Grant had mother's approval now, and that meant the others felt more free to talk to him. All the same, I'd told Grant to be careful what he said and did. He's really under a kind of probation, and I don't want him to mess it up.

Later on, I got talking with Dawn. We were on a sofa in a quiet corner, nice and private.

Dawn said, "Grant's the perfect gentleman today. Is that all down to what Ben did?"

I laughed. "Partly, but I thought about what you said that time, that Grant should respect me, not just Ben. So I had a little game with him, playing a dominatrix. That shocked him. He didn't expect it at all."

"So what did you do?"

"I'm not going into all the details, but well, I made him do things. It's funny, but once I'd dressed up, and used the whip —"

Her eyes widened. "A whip? Oh my God, I wish I'd been there. Did he let you do it?"

"He had no choice. He was in handcuffs."

"Good Lord, that sounds exciting. Did he like it?"

I shook my head. "He was trying to get me to stop. I made him call me mistress, and in the end he was begging 'please, mistress'. It sounds comical, but I know I frightened him."

"No wonder he's more compliant. And what were you wearing?"

"I was all in black, and had a black wig. I looked very erotic."

"I'll bet you did … I wouldn't mind seeing you in that outfit."

I laughed. "Then I might decide to tie you up, and make you do things too."

She whispered. "There'll be no need to tie me up, … mistress."

"You might get more than you expect. Now come on, it's time to go. Let's see what the boys are up to."

In the back room, Grant and Robin were with my brothers, talking sport.

Ben's sometimes hostile towards Grant, and vice versa, but there seemed less tension today.

I said, "We're ready to go."

Grant and Robin stood up, still in conversation.

Robin said, "Baseball's my favorite. At school, I used to be a pretty good pitcher. What about you, Frank?"

"I was in the school team, but I liked to bat, and I was the best. That year, the school won the —"

Ben interrupted, "The others don't want to hear all that."

Dawn and I kissed our brothers goodbye, and turned to go.

But Grant had a puzzled expression, and turned back. "You'll have to tell us more sometime, but Frank, do you still have your bat?"

"Sure do. It's a beauty. Aluminum, and with the team signatures on it. I'll show it to you sometime."

It was on the way back that I asked Grant, "What was that about the baseball bat?"

"Oh, I was just curious. That guy was beaten to death, and the detectives thought it was an aluminum bat that was used."

I laughed. "Well, it wouldn't be Frank's. He treats that as if it was made of gold. You'll be lucky if he even lets you touch it."

"I guessed that. And I know it's only a coincidence."

# 39

When I got home from work, April had already got the meal ready, some microwave pasta, and was putting it out on the table.

I said, "We're eating early, aren't we?"

She smiled but said nothing. Then she ate like it was a race. When she'd finished, and I was still halfway through, she stood up.

"I'm going out tonight, so I had to get dinner out of the way. Now I must go and change."

And off she went to her bedroom.

I'd assumed it was another business meeting. But when she came back, I knew differently. A dress almost short enough to be indecent. High heels. Jewelry. And impeccable makeup.

"It's not a company event then?"

She paused, as if deciding what she would tell me.

"I've a date."

If she'd said that just after we got married, I'd have thought I misheard. But I was used to her now.

"What am I supposed to say to that? We're married. You shouldn't talk of dates."

"Why not? It's the truth. Shouldn't we be honest with each other?"

"So where does that leave me?"

"You're my husband. Nothing changes about that. Scott's got a party invite, and he needs a partner, to take with him. And as he's broken up with his girlfriend, tonight I'm filling in."

"Doesn't that make you his girlfriend?"

"Maybe it does, for this evening."

"Hell, April, that's how marriages break up."

"Not ours. You're my perfect husband, and I wouldn't swap you for Scott or anyone else. But as a boyfriend, Scott's fun, at least for now."

"Great, so I sit here watching the TV and you're out somewhere with Scott. What time will you be back?"

"The party goes on until the early hours, so I won't be back tonight. I'll go to Scott's afterwards to freshen up before I go to work tomorrow morning. Anyway, darling, I must go. I don't want to be late."

And then she was gone. All too fast to take in, never mind raising an objection. I got a beer, and watched the TV for a while. But I couldn't concentrate. She was annoying, with her matter-of-fact logic about having a date. The situation was ridiculous, but she didn't see that, and nothing I said mattered. It was so obvious that she was going to sleep with him, after the party. But if I'd asked, she'd have denied it. Or worse still, she'd have said yes, and given me another of her ridiculous explanations.

There was a knock at the door.

I wasn't expecting anyone, so opened it cautiously. It was Dawn. And dressed as scantily as April. But not so cute. More like a hooker.

She smiled. "Want some company?" and brushed past me, carrying a large bag.

I said, "April's out."

"I know that. That's why I'm here. I didn't want you sad and lonely on your own."

She came close and kissed me. After our night in Vegas, I'd been wondering if we might get back together. The evening was looking more interesting already.

"What about Robin?"

"He's fine on his own."

I said, "What's in the bag?"

"Oh, overnight things."

I stuttered, "You mean you're staying the night?"

"April's not going to be back, so it's worked out well for all of us. Are you pleased?"

"But what if April finds out?"

Dawn laughed. "You are naive sometimes."

143

# 40

Robin asked me the other day if things were working out with April.

"It's not the way I expected it to be, but I've got used to her strange ways. So overall, I'd say things are pretty good."

"And you seem to be fitting in with the family now, especially with their mother. It was difficult for me to start with, but I know it was harder for you."

"The family's okay. Except for her brothers. And Ben's weird. The less I have to do with him the better."

I wondered if Robin knew the detail of my encounters with Ben. April will have told her sister everything, but Dawn wouldn't necessarily have told Robin.

Robin smiled. "And we all get on well don't we? The four of us here in the same block?"

It was only a week ago that this poor guy slept alone, while Dawn spent the night with me. Yet he talks as if it didn't happen. Maybe that's the way he is.

"I guess we do get on. The only downside is that the girls have too much time together plotting their little schemes. And we have to go along with it all."

"Like the vacation in Vegas? But that wasn't bad was it?"

"I'm not saying it's bad. But I wish we were consulted before they make their decisions."

Robin shrugged. "I'm happy enough with it all. Life's simpler if I leave it to Dawn to decide things."

"Maybe you're right. I can't really complain."

"So, Grant, what does the future hold?"

That was a good question.

April will probably tire of having Scott as her boyfriend, although maybe then she'll replace him with another one.

Her career will progress, one way or another.

April and Dawn will no doubt keep Robin and me guessing. But if it means sleeping with Dawn from time to time, then I'm all for it.

And where does that leave me? Anyone seeing us at home would say April's like a queen bee, and I'm becoming submissive, just as Robin is with Dawn. But I'm happy enough with the way things are. As Robin says, it makes life simpler.

And in a strange way, it makes April more desirable.

Robin was waiting for an answer.

I smiled. "The future? You'll have to ask April."

# Part 8 – THE BOYFRIEND MOVES IN

## 41

~ ~ ~ ~ *Grant* ~ ~ ~ ~

Dawn closed the door behind her.

"So, Grant, how long have we got?"

If this had happened months ago, I'd have been lost for words. But I was used to the ways of April's sister by now.

"She'll be an hour or so, no more than two."

She put her arms around my neck and pulled me towards her.

I kissed her, inhaling her perfume.

I love April more than anyone, but this woman is irresistible.

~ ~ ~ ~ *April* ~ ~ ~ ~

I was always happy to go shopping with Dawn. After all, that's what sisters are for. And we've a favorite place to have coffee, and watch the world go by.

Dawn said, "So April, is Grant your perfect husband yet?"

"He always has been. The only problem early on was his selfish attitude to things I wanted. He was usually as good as gold, but then sometimes he'd argue with me, and push to get his own way. It was so tiresome, but he's a lot better now, and he hardly argues at all. It did need help from our brothers, but you know about that."

146

"I'm still not sure you should have got Ben involved. He always had a tendency to violence, even when he was young. And the beatings he gave Grant, and especially what he and Frank did last time, it must have been so humiliating."

"It was rather horrible, wasn't it? Men can be so bestial. But then maybe the results justify it. And anyway, I don't need Ben now. Grant is wary of me too, after our little game."

Dawn leaned forward. "You wouldn't really harm him while he's asleep, would you?"

"He believes it, that's the important thing."

"So when are you going to let me have another night with him?"

"Dawn, it's not going to be a regular thing, so you'll have to wait. You've got Robin, anyway. You'll have to work out your passions with him."

"Oh, he's okay, but I like a change. And Grant's so powerful. I love that feeling once in a while to be held by a man that I can't stop. Not that I'd want him to. You're not planning another night away with your boyfriend then?"

"Not right now. But in any case, if I do go away for the night, it doesn't mean you automatically get Grant each time."

Dawn looked subdued, so I put my hand across to hold hers.

"Oh, Dawn, if Robin's not enough, can't you find someone else to spend the night with? Does it have to be Grant? What about that salesman you were seeing?"

"I'm bored with him. Of course, there is one person I enjoy sleeping with, almost as much as Grant, isn't there?"

I didn't respond, but couldn't help smile.

We were on the way back to our apartment building, when I asked, "Dawn, what do you know about our father?"

"Not much. Why the sudden interest?"

"Grant was asking me, and it made me realize how little I know. Mother never talks about him, so it's not a topic to bring up. I know his name, and what's on our birth certificates. But that's it."

"He came from Oregon, some place down in the south of the state. Near Medford, wasn't it? Maybe he went back there. But it's not always a good idea to poke around this sort of thing. He might be a horrible man, and he might not want to see any of us. I'd forget it."

"Grant's more interested than I am. I suppose that's because his own parents are dead, and maybe he's intrigued."

Dawn shook her head. "Well, tell him to stop. I don't want some creepy old man coming round and wanting to be friends."

"Why should he be creepy? He might be nice, and wishing he'd been able to keep in touch."

"You know, Ben did a bit of research once. Quite a few years back."

"I don't remember that."

"He kept it quiet. He only told me because I saw some printout he had. But he didn't get anywhere, and had to give up."

"I suppose Grant could ask Ben, but they're barely on speaking terms. And I'm not that interested."

Dawn frowned. "Best not to ask anyway. He might get angry with me for telling about it."

"He'd forgive you. We're about the only people he cares for."

"More you than me. He's infatuated with you."

I'd never told Dawn the whole truth, and wasn't about to now.


~ ~ ~ ~ *Grant* ~ ~ ~ ~


I'd had a good workout at the gym. The steroids and the exercise are coming together, adding about ten pounds to my body weight, and it's all upper body muscle. The downside is that the steroids seem to be boosting my libido, and it's almost painful not to be able to do something about it, especially when the women at the gym show interest in me. I don't get it often enough with April, and at times, I'd fuck anything, never mind the women.

Robin has started coming to the gym now. He does his own thing. Not surprising, as next to me, in his spandex, he looks like a skinny little woman.

At home, April was back already.

"Good shopping trip with Dawn?"

"Yes, fine. I didn't buy anything though. Most of the time we sat and chatted."

"Did you ask about your father?"

"I did, but she knew no more than me. And she's not keen on finding out."

"But you're interested to know, aren't you?"

"I'm in two minds. I'm curious, but I'm nervous too, about what might get uncovered. So as Dawn's against it, I think we'll leave things as they are."

I was even more curious than her. To me the attitude of the whole family was puzzling. Now I'd got to know them, I was finding out more, but there was never a mention of the father. I could understand it if he'd been a criminal, or if he'd beaten April's mother or the children. But there wasn't even a hint of that. I'd have to investigate on my own, and take it carefully.

I laughed. "Hey, in your discussion, there was no mention of swapping again?"

"No, not for now. Anyway, you got more out of it than I did."

"But you said you liked sleeping with Robin."

"That's true. He was nice. By the way, there is something I need to tell you. I've got Scott coming to stay for a few days."

"What for?"

"He's moving apartments, and he needs somewhere to stay. So as we've a spare room, —"

"Is that where he'll be sleeping?"

Her expression tensed up. "It irritates me when you try to be clever with me. So stop doing that. And as for your question, he'll sleep where I tell him. Just as you do."

"Isn't it going to cause gossip in the office, what with you being his manager?"

"They can gossip all they want. I always find out who's been doing the talking, and I deal with it when the time's right."

"You can't fire them for talking about you."

"Grant, darling, it's more subtle that that. I don't rush things. At review time, I'll mark them down, for something judgmental. Nothing they can appeal against."

"They must wonder what they have with you. Cute one minute, then the flip side, settling scores."

"If they've any sense, they've got used to me by now."

"That doesn't mean they like it."

# 42

On Friday after work, Scott arrived, and took over the spare room. I'd made the bed, and in his bedside cupboard drawer, I'd put a photo of me, in my bikini. Better than finding a bible.

I was pleased to have him staying, but the evening had felt uncomfortable, with the three of us watching TV together. I sat with Scott on the sofa, and occasionally we shared some joke or gossip about the office. Grant was across the room in a chair, a bit sulky, probably feeling as though he was the odd one out. Still, I always think it's important to make guests feel at ease.

Lying in bed later, I did wonder if I'd get a late night visit, and I stayed awake for a while. But he didn't come. Perhaps it was just as well, as he'd have had to come past Grant's room, and Grant was sure to be listening out.

Early on Saturday morning, Grant got a phone call from where he worked. They had a new rush order, and so he had to go in there for the day. That worked out well, as it gave me time with Scott, so after breakfast I suggested we go shopping.

He's younger than me, and I didn't want to make it look as if I had a toy boy, so I dressed young. Tight T-shirt, jeans and pink trainers, and even an Alice band in my hair. He couldn't stop smiling when he saw me, and I knew I'd got it right. When he sees me at work, I'm his boss, and I'm dressed for the office, but in this outfit it feels different for me, and now I know it does for him too.

At the mall, we headed towards a coffee shop. I felt like a teenager with him.

"Scott, forget the office today. Hold my hand."

151

We walked along hand in hand, and by the time we got there, his arm was round my shoulder. We found a dark corner to drink our coffee.

"Scott, have you got a new girlfriend?"

"No. Why do you ask?"

"I think of myself as your girlfriend now, and I wouldn't want competition. Especially if we're going to be having fun together the next few days."

"But what about Grant?"

"He's my husband, but that doesn't mean I can't have a boyfriend. He'll not be a problem."

"I don't know. He's a big guy, and I wouldn't want to cross him."

"I already stayed the night with you, and he's not given you any trouble so far, has he?"

His eyes went wide. "He knows about that?"

"Of course."

Scott looked thoughtful. "I'm still nervous about him. What if he's stacking things up, and then —"

"He's not going to do that. Anyway, I can deal with any trouble. So for now, I'm your girlfriend. And that means I'm available whenever you want, especially at night."

"I don't know."

I leaned over the table to him and pouted slightly. "Scott, at least kiss me."

He glanced around, then kissed me. Hesitantly, like a teenage kiss. He was hooked.

"Now you're my official boyfriend, and that's final. So let's go back home. I want to know what sort of things you've done with your other girlfriends, and I'll want the same at least."

When I got back on Saturday, it was early evening.

Before I entered the living room, I could hear the two of them giggling about something, like kids. So that was the way it was. She was going to be all over him while he was here, and I would be a bystander. More or less what I expected.

When I went in, she looked relaxed, and smiled, but Scott sat upright, and his smile was strained. He muttered something about checking his emails, and went off to his room, leaving me with April.

"So, have you had a good day with Scott?"

"It was lovely. We went shopping this morning, and we've been here after that, watching TV, and enjoying each other's company."

"What does that mean exactly?"

She laughed. "Nothing you need to know about."

"Well, I think he's too intimate with you, given that you're his manager."

"Oh, we don't think about that. While he's here, I've told him to be informal, and forget work. I've said he should treat this as his home, and to think of me as a friend, in fact as his girlfriend."

"What?"

"You heard. His girlfriend. It makes him feel more at home. And anyway, when you're not around, it's fun for me to pretend to have a boyfriend."

"So how far does the pretense go?"

"As far as I want. Now stop interrogating me. You're behaving like a policeman."

"Maybe I should have a girlfriend too?"

"That's stupid. You've got me, and that should be enough. I suppose you're thinking of Dawn?"

"Not particularly. But I get frustrated going to bed on my own. If I can't sleep with you, then why not Dawn?"

April's usually so angelic, but her expression gets vicious when she gets mad. And now she was mad.

"If you're going to talk that way, then you'd better go to your room. And if you're that frustrated, you'll have to masturbate."

I was in my room when they went to bed. No pretense this time. They'd been drinking, and I could hear them laughing as they went to her bedroom, and closed the door. I tried to shut out the noise, but they were making no effort to be quiet. It must have been an hour or so before they finished, and I got to sleep.

# 43

~ ~ ~ ~ *April* ~ ~ ~ ~

Scott has been with us for a week now, and it's been a mixed experience. I love having him around, but Grant gets so moody about it. He hardly talks to Scott, and doesn't say much more to me. It creates an unpleasant atmosphere, and it's so unnecessary.

Scott has been sleeping with me, which was fun to start with, although it's getting a bit repetitive. The main problem is me. I'm not used to having sex so frequently, and I prefer sleeping on my own anyway.

Scott is happy enough with the sleeping arrangements, except that he's still nervous about possible repercussions. I've told him Grant's sulking and it doesn't mean anything, but he's got into his mind that he might suddenly boil over and go for him. It's so frustrating. They could easily be friends, but they hardly even communicate.

So I've come up with a plan, and in the evening I told them.

"Listen, the atmosphere's been uncomfortable the last few days, and it can't go on. So I've made a decision to bring things to a head. Tonight, I want you both in bed next to me, Grant on one side, and Scott on the other."

Grant's mouth fell open. "You can't mean that —"

"Every word. I want you both next to me, and for us all to get on together."

"I won't have it. You can sleep with him all you like, but I'm not sharing the bed with you both."

I guessed he might object, and I'd meant to keep calm, but his attitude was so inflexible, that I lost my temper.

I found myself shouting. "You'll do what I say!"

Scott finally spoke, "April, I'm not keen either. Maybe I should be in my own room tonight."

I turned on him. "Oh, are you getting bored with me?"

He stuttered, "No, I —"

"Right, then I've changed my mind. I'll sleep on my own tonight."

I stormed out of the living room and slammed the door.

~ ~ ~ ~ *Grant* ~ ~ ~ ~

It all happened so fast that I lost track. First her crazy suggestion, then a load of angry shouting, and then she was gone. I went to the drinks cabinet and got out a couple of glasses.

I turned to Scott, who was looking pale and confused. "Whiskey?"

I handed him the glass and sat opposite. "Cheer up, Scott. She'll have forgotten it in the morning."

"I've not seen her shouting like that, even at the office. She's scary."

He took a gulp of the whiskey.

I sat back. "She can get worse than that, believe me. It's as if she switches on a different personality. Right now, she'll be seething, but I know her well enough. She won't come out again tonight, so it'll be peaceful in here." I raised my glass. "Cheers."

He broke into a smile and sipped some more. "Anything on the TV?"

"No, don't think so. But I've got the highlights of the last Super Bowl."

It was mid-morning before I got dressed and went to the kitchen. April and Scott were finishing breakfast, looking once more that they were the couple here.

Scott said to me, "Are you okay?"

"Yeah, fine. I slept well."

Scott moved his eyebrows slightly. He was good at subtle messages. So he'd slept well too. Not surprising as he'd had his first night without fucking my wife.

I looked at April. "And how are you this morning, dear?"

"I'm all right, but you two did annoy me. I want us all to get on together, and I'd put a lot of thought into it. Then you both dismissed it out of hand."

"But we do get on well enough, considering the situation we're in."

I looked at Scott for support, but he kept quiet. Can't blame him.

I said to April, "So what happens next?"

She brightened up. "It's a good plan, and I'm sure it will work out, if we all try our best. Maybe I rushed things. So today, we're all going out together, and we're going to be friends. Then this evening, we'll have dinner here with a glass or two of champagne, and then I really will have both of you sleep with me. And no sex. I just want us all to get on. That's surely not too much to ask."


~ ~ ~ ~ *April* ~ ~ ~ ~


I turned the bedside light off. Finally I had them both with me, all of us naked. I'd never been in bed with two men, and I was tingling. I felt so desirable, having two men of my own.

I'd dreamed last night about it. Or maybe fantasized. I imagined that they argued over who should have me, and then started wrestling, both naked. But tonight the reality was good enough, feeling them next to me. They were lying on their backs, keeping quiet. Probably nervous about what I might suggest.

I put my hands out, and touched them, and moved down slowly until I had a hand on each of them. They both had gone stiff. So predictable. I could do what I wanted with them.

I said, "You're both nice to touch, and I would have sex, but I've had enough of that, the last few days. So let's just lie here."

I could feel that they were both tense, but as the minutes went by, they relaxed.

I said, "This is how I imagined it. Lying here with my wonderful husband and my new boyfriend. I'm glad we're all friends now. So Grant, will you give me a good night kiss?"

Grant leaned towards me and kissed me. Not his best kiss, but under the circumstances it was probably as good as I was going to get.

"Now Scott, you kiss me goodnight."

Scott's kiss was worse than Grant's. He's scared of Grant, and that's not helping.

We'd been lying there for a couple of minutes, when I had an idea.

"Listen, are you two friends now?"

They both muttered an unenthusiastic yes.

"Then Grant, I want you to lean across me and give Scott a kiss too."

"But April, …"

He might have been objecting, but I still had hold of him, and felt his penis going hard again. Scott's too. Men are funny.

"No arguments this time. It won't hurt you. So do it, and we can all go to sleep. Now kiss him, and I mean properly, on the lips."

Grant muttered some complaint, but then he leaned over me and I heard the kiss.

# 44

Scott's new apartment was ready, and he'd be moving in tomorrow, so it was his last night with us. He's a nice enough guy, but it would be a relief to see him gone. She'd only slept with him once since our threesome, but that was little consolation, as while she had him around, my own sex was on hold.

If that wasn't bad enough, this morning April told me of her latest idea.

She'd wanted to make Scott's last night special. I'd already assumed she'd be sleeping with him, but she wanted more than that. After dinner, she planned to go to her bedroom with him, and watch a movie together in bed. And to cap it all, I was to bring them drinks during the evening. I grumbled that it was making me into a servant, but she saw no problem with that.

So with dinner over, they went to the bedroom. Before long came my first call. When I entered, they were on the bed, sitting at the far end, propped up with pillows. She was wearing a flimsy baby-doll nightie, and he was in his briefs.

"Grant, darling, you can bring us a couple of glasses of wine now."

I got two more calls for drinks, but the next call was different. This time the lights were low, and they were both naked. Scott had an erection.

"Darling, a little job for you, I'm sure you don't mind. But first, take your clothes off."

I stripped off, and stood there, with Scott looking pale and nervous.

April said, "Now unwrap one of Scott's condoms. They're on the cupboard."

159

I took the condom out of its wrapper, and handed it towards him.

She interrupted me. "Grant, it's his special night. Put it on for him."

Scott was looking really worried now. I gave her as furious an expression as I could. But she gave me one of her "Don't annoy me" looks. At least it would all be finished with by tomorrow.

I leaned over Scott, and rolled it onto his penis.

It should have felt humiliating or at least embarrassing, but I'm so used to April's crazy ways, it was just one more thing. For Scott, it was another matter. His face had gone pink, and he held his breath while I was doing it. I could see him suffering, so I took a bit longer than I needed.

He drew a deep breath when it was done.

She looked at us both, "Very good. Now Grant, I've got to give Scott his goodbye treat. Go and sit over there, and you can watch."

It was too much for Scott, "You surely don't want him to stay here?"

"That's exactly what I want. It'll make it more exciting for us."

"But I don't know if I can, with Grant watching."

She laughed. "I'm sure you'll manage. After a little while you'll forget he's here."

Then she started on the poor guy.

He didn't forget that I was there. Every now and then I saw a furtive glance in my direction. He took a long time to get his erection back, and then he never climaxed. But April was enjoying the whole thing. She too would look over at me occasionally.

I watched it like it was a movie. The fact that April was my wife didn't matter. It was fascinating watching her perform with him, and him bouncing around on top of her. His body was so slim, the same as Robin's. At times, from behind, I could believe I was watching two women.

When they had finished, they both lay there in silence. Then April said, "Grant, you can go to your room now. But a goodnight kiss first please."

I went over to her and kissed her. Then turned to go. But I could guess what was coming.

She said, "Now kiss Scott."

When my lips made contact, I could taste April's lipstick. That made it easier. And I knew he would hate it, so I made it last.

# Part 9 – A LESBIAN EXPERIENCE

# 45

*~ ~ ~ ~ April ~ ~ ~ ~*

The club wasn't busy. The background music was at a low volume, and there were only a dozen or so women there. But it was interesting all the same.

"You know, Dawn, it still seems surreal to see women kissing each other in public. Not that there's anything wrong with it."

Dawn laughed. "So long as the women aren't ugly."

I sipped my cocktail. "That was a lovely movie. And it's nice to go somewhere afterwards, but why do you like it so much here?"

"No particular reason. It's a nice atmosphere, and it gives us something to look at. And there's no rush to be back, is there?"

"No. The boys will be happy enough watching sports on the TV, so they won't care if we're late. But let's stick together. I don't want to end up dancing with some butch type in denim."

Dawn squeezed my hand. "Don't worry. I'll look after you. Now what's happening with Grant? Have things settled down again, now Scott's gone?"

"Oh, he was huffy for a while, but a couple of nights with me, and he's back to normal."

"You should have let him stay with me while you had Scott there."

"I'd never have got him back. As it was, he was talking about you."

Dawn smiled. "Was he now? You've made my day. But now I'll be dreaming about him, and it'll get frustrating. So can't we swap again sometime? Maybe when we all go to San Francisco for the weekend?"

"I told you before, you can't have him anytime you want. Anyway, we haven't decided yet about San Francisco. And if we do go, I don't know if I want to do any swapping. I'm not sure I get as good a deal with these swaps as you do. Robin's nice, but —"

"There's nothing wrong with Robin. But I need a change once in a while. Now if you'd let me have Grant for one night?"

"If you want a change, find someone else."

Dawn went quiet, and sipped her drink. Then she looked up. "What about you? I'd settle for a night with you, April."

She's very sensuous, and I did enjoy sleeping with her. All the same, she had an orgasm, and I didn't. But I had an idea.

"You want to sleep with me, and play around like last time?"

She was smiling, "Yes, it was good fun wasn't it?"

"All right, but with one condition. Before you get your night, I want mine. I want to play a dominatrix again, just as I did with Grant, but this time you'll be my submissive."

"I don't know about that. Would you have the whip?"

"It's part of the outfit, part of my persona."

"But when you did that with Grant, you hurt him. You said so yourself."

"That's because I was teaching him a lesson. I'd not hit you hard. Little flicks, that's all, if you don't behave properly."

"What if I do behave?"

"Nobody's perfect. I'll have to give you a little flick at some point. That's what a dominatrix does."

"I don't know. I've never done that kind of thing before, and it's a bit scary thinking about it. I don't want to be tied up, and I'm not sure I trust you, after what you did to Grant."

"But if you do that for me, then you get your night, and you can play your little games. Whatever you want to do with me. I'll have to trust you too."

Dawn looked miserable. I knew she was tempted, but I'd told her too much about what I'd done to Grant. Her eyes were wandering, looking round enviously at the couples nearby. She wasn't going to agree, and I did want to play my own game with her. The more I thought about it, the more I wanted it.

Dawn said, "I do trust you, but —"

I leaned forward, close to her. "If you do this for me, I'll do something extra special."

Her eyes looked hopeful. "You mean more than a night together?"

"We'll go to San Francisco for a weekend, without the men. In the daytime, we'll walk around as lovers, like the women in here, holding hands and kissing. And then at night, we'll do whatever you want. And that'll be two days and nights. What do you say?"

### ~ ~ ~ ~ *Grant* ~ ~ ~ ~

"How long do you think we've got, Robin?"

"They'll be hours. Dawn said they'll be going for a drink, after the movie."

"So where do we start? You're the expert."

"Hardly that. I've done some family history research, that's all. Anyway, we start with the details on Dawn's birth certificate, and do some searches."

Robin got busy on his laptop, searching Oregon indexes, and I left him to it.

After an hour, and two beers, Robin said. "It's not been that easy. I've an index entry that seems to match, so we can request a copy of his birth certificate. But their rules mean we have to prove our connection before they'll issue it. And we don't want anyone to know what we're doing."

"Hell, no. April would go mad if she knew."

"So I'm not sure what to try next. The usual thing would be to check the marriage details, but I for one aren't going to ask their mother to see her certificate. Maybe you could, now she thinks you're so wonderful."

"Hardly that, I only fixed her air con. Anyway, it was just an idea. I was interested to know more about him, but I guess he might be dead anyway."

Robin leaned forward to the keyboard. "Now that's a thought. I could check the death records."

After a few minutes, "This could be him. Ten years ago, and in his original home town. But again, I've only the index. If it's him, he certainly died young."

Robin tapped away again.

I asked, "What are you trying now?"

"If the death was unusual, it might have been reported in the local newspaper, or it could be in the obituaries. I'm doing a search. Ah, here it is."

It was an old news item on the screen. It was April's father, as the name and age matched, as well as the locality. He had been murdered, by persons unknown.

I looked at Robin. "How can we see the whole story?"

"It's not on the internet. You'd have to go there and look through the archived copies at the publisher, or maybe the local library."

"Maybe I should leave well alone. We can't tell April and Dawn anyway."

"But it's intriguing, isn't it? I mean, how did he die? And who were the suspects? Not that I'd be that interested to do a road trip to find out."

I said, "They might not even keep the old copies, so it could be a wasted journey."

Robin tapped the keys. "It wouldn't be wasted. The library there has the old copies on microfilm. The full article might have all sorts of information. Maybe an address. And if you follow through the newspaper issues after that, you might find more mentions."

I looked again at the extract on the screen.

Murdered. By persons unknown.

# 46

It was exciting getting dressed, with Dawn watching me, sitting there naked, and looking increasingly nervous.

I dressed the same as for Grant. Corset, stockings, and high heels. All black. And my long black wig. I applied the lipstick, and checked in the mirror.

Whether it was the way the corset squeezed me, or the excitement of the moment, my nipples seemed huge, poking out from their openings. As a finishing touch, I put a little lipstick on them too.

"Well, Dawn, I'm ready."

I picked up the whip, and turned to face her.

"What do you think?"

"You look so erotic. Even a bit intimidating. So what do you want me to wear?"

"Only one thing."

I got it from the cupboard. A white leather collar, on a leash.

Dawn's eyes widened. "What's that? I said I didn't want to be tied up."

"It's a collar with a leash. It's symbolic, that you're my submissive. Now let me put it on."

I looped it over her head, and pulled the leash to tighten it.

"Ouch! That's hurting."

"That's because you're pulling away from me. It's a slip knot, and it tightens up if you do that."

I stood back, and pulled gently on the leash, making her head move involuntarily. Perfect. She was mine now.

I turned down the lights, to make the atmosphere more seductive. Then I stood facing her.

167

"Come over to me."

Dawn stood, and faced me. She's slightly taller than me, but in my heels, I was looking down on her. A weird feeling. She wasn't my big sister now. She was my submissive.

"Kiss me, then down on your knees."

Dawn kissed me hesitantly, and then knelt down below me.

I took hold of the leash, then flicked her with the whip.

She said, "Why did you do that?"

"I was testing. And you must call me mistress, every time you speak. Now say you're sorry."

"Sorry for what?"

I pulled the leash tight, then swung the whip down hard on her.

"Ouch. That hurt."

She tried to stand up, but I held her down with the leash.

"Dawn, you're not doing it right. You must call me mistress. Now say you're sorry."

She was silent, then she looked up at me and in a low voice, "I'm sorry, mistress."

"That's better."

I leaned down and kissed her. She'd do anything for that weekend away. So tonight I could do what I wanted. But I had to reward her occasionally.

"Now a game. You're to be a little piglet. On your hands and knees."

"Do I have to? ... mistress?"

I held the leash tight, and struck her again with the whip.

Then I shouted, "Don't challenge me! You do what I say, or you get punished."

She got on her hands and knees.

I pinched her on the buttock, and heard a little noise from her. Then I stroked her buttocks and thighs. "You're a little piggy now. Will you be a good piggy?"

"Yes, mistress."

"So let's see how well you can walk around. If you go too fast, I'll pull on the leash. But if you go too slow, I'll have to whip you."

She said, "Please don't whip me. It hurts."

I struck her hard on the buttocks, and shouted, "Mistress! You must say mistress."

She struggled, and I held the leash firm, but it was difficult, as she's stronger than me. But in the end, she was choking herself and coughing, and had to stop struggling.

"Dawn, if you keep trying to do that, I'm going to whip you over and over, and pull your collar really tight."

The poor thing started crying. She looked so pathetic, on the floor, on my leash, and I felt so powerful. As children and as teenagers, she'd always been the one in charge, but now here I was. I looked over at the mirror. I was standing above her, tall and strong, and she was on the floor, crying. She really was my submissive now. It was better than with Grant.

I let her finish crying, then, "Right, Dawn, are you ready?"

"Yes, mistress."

She started crawling along, and as she did, I gave the leash a little tug once in a while, and flicked the whip on her buttocks. We went round the bedroom twice, and she'd have gone on longer, but it was getting boring.

"Okay, Dawn, we've finished that game. Now you can get back on your knees."

Her eyes were red from the crying, but the tears had dried. Good, she'd be ready for the next stage.

I stood in front of her and strapped on the dildo, adjusting the straps carefully, so that it felt firm and secure.

"Now Dawn, what do you think of my penis?"

"It's big, mistress. Very big."

"Suck it. As if it's on a man."

She came forward and put her lips around it, and started sucking.

While she did that, I leaned down, and started stroking her breasts. Larger than mine. But just as firm. And she was getting excited, sucking harder than she needed to.

"Dawn, you can stop that."

I pulled on the leash, and brought her to stand facing me.

"Tell me how you'd like to kiss your mistress."

"I'd kiss you softly, mistress, and then I'd put my tongue between your lips."

"Then do it, bitch."

She kissed me beautifully. Exactly as she'd said, softly, and delicately.

I used the leash to pull her back away from my face.

"Now lie on the bed, on your back."

She looked nervous. "What are you going to do, mistress?"

"Can't you guess?"

As I got onto the bed, and moved to mount her, she moved her legs apart, and raised her knees. I hadn't expected her to be so compliant. She was tense, but she was excited too. Even in the low light, I could see that her face was flushed and I could hear her breathing becoming intense.

Yet I felt calm. No sexual arousal like her. But a feeling of power, knowing what I was about to do to her.

I leaned down and kissed her. "You're mine now, aren't you, bitch?"

She stuttered, "Yes, mistress."

I pushed my penis into her, ever so gently. Her mouth opened, and her breathing became deeper and faster. I kissed her nipples in turn, then started alternately pushing into her, and relaxing back. I had to think it step by step to start with, but the rhythm soon became natural.

She had her hands on me now, feeling my nipples, through the openings in the corset. They were so sensitive, that I could feel every touch. I was feeling hot, and my body was moving with hers now. This woman was mine, and I

170

was making love to her just as Grant would. Maybe better. I wasn't rushing anything.

Her breathing was unsteady, and almost in gasps now, and her body was making small involuntary movements. I let myself go with it, and stopped thinking about anything but my own feelings. With one last push into her, she screamed out in pleasure, and my own body shook. I dropped down on her and kissed her over and over.

She started sobbing again, but this time it was because she was happy. I kissed the tears on her cheeks, and her watery eyes opened wide, looking into mine.

She said, "You were wonderful, mistress."

I had to smile. "You don't have to call me that any more. I think you've done enough."

She pouted, and I leaned down to kiss her. I do love my sister.

We'd been lying next to each other for a while afterwards, and we'd both calmed down.

I'd taken the penis off, but I was still in my outfit. A dominatrix lying next to the naked body of her submissive. I loved the feeling, but it was time to finish.

I started to remove her collar, but she put her hand up to stop me.

She whispered, "What else can I do for you, mistress?"

# 47

I hate shopping with April, but it's even worse on my own. I don't know where anything is in the mall, and I go back and forth to get every item.

I was ready for lunch, when I met Ben and his mother.

She said, "Shopping, Grant? Without April?"

"She's gone into the office today, for some special meeting. So she gave me a list, and here I am. I'm going to grab something to eat at the food court, and then I'm done."

"Well, it's kind of handy you're here. Ben's had a phone call and has to go, so could you take me back home?"

"Of course. Do you want to go now?"

"No rush. I could have lunch too."

Ben muttered something about his call, then left.

She smiled. "But not the food court. It's always crowded on Saturday. Let's go to the Italian restaurant, and have something special. My treat."

She's so different, away from the rest of the family. A different woman, and looking ten years younger, almost like an older sister for April and Dawn. And she's kept her figure.

Italian food's all right, but it's too fussy. I'd prefer a burger and fries in the food court, but she loves the stuff. And with a glass of wine, I was beginning to warm to the cuisine. We started talking about April, then onto Dawn and the brothers. It's strange. She rattles on about how they were as kids, and then as suddenly, she cuts off and changes the subject. As if she'd been about to stray onto something that she doesn't want me to know.

We got on well, over that meal. So I thought I'd take a chance.

"I have a question, and you may not want to answer it, so I'm wary of asking."

"I'm intrigued. Go on. I won't be offended whatever it is."

"It's about April's father. I wondered what became of him?"

She shrugged. "It's no concern of mine. We split up long ago, and I've never tried to contact him. No doubt he's got his own life now, but I'm not interested."

"So there's been no attempt to find out?"

"Ben talked about it some years back, but he's no researcher, and he soon gave up. And as far as I know, April and Dawn have no interest."

"And I don't suppose Frank …?"

"Of course not."

My hands were on the table. She reached across, and put her hands on mine. "Forget the past, Grant. Live for the present. That's what I do."

"I guess so. And you're right. April's got no interest."

"How's she treating you these days? Is she a good wife?"

"Yes, I'm lucky to have her."

She smiled at me, and squeezed my hands. "She's lucky to have you. You're quite a man."

She stared into my eyes. "If you were single, I wouldn't care about the age difference. I'd try flirting with you."

I laughed, and responded without thinking. "And if I were single, I'd be pleased if you did. You're a beautiful woman."

She let go of my hands. I might have overstepped it, but she could hardly blame me. I'd had two glasses of wine, and she'd said what she said.

We chatted a bit more, about the shops and what was in the news, and then it was time to take her home. It was hardly a word said, while we were driving back. She was busy checking her emails or messages on her smartphone.

I pulled up onto the driveway, shaded with trees and quite private. I was expecting her to get out of the car.

"Grant, come closer. I've something to say."

I leaned towards her, and she smiled. "It was a nice compliment you gave me. It's a long time since anyone said I was beautiful."

She came closer to me, until my face was right against hers. I was breathing in her perfume, and it was intoxicating.

Then she kissed me.

Barely a touch on the lips. But a kiss all the same.


~ ~ ~ ~ *April* ~ ~ ~ ~


It was a nuisance having to go in on Saturday, but I knew what it was about. I've enough friends to keep me informed.

In front of his door, I took a deep breath. The vice-president of Operations was important to my career, and I'd got him annoyed.

The VP looked up from his desk. "I called you in this morning, because I wanted to talk to you off the record, without anyone seeing you here and speculating. It's about your man Scott."

Best to play the innocent. "Has he done something wrong?"

"No, it's not that. It's the way he got appointed. There have been complaints."

"But he was the best person for the job. What's wrong with that?"

"You know damned well. There's a procedure here, and you bypassed it. You didn't even advertise the job internally."

"He was acting manager, and he was doing a good job. So what would be the point of all that? He'd have been appointed anyway."

174

"Maybe, but at least it would have followed procedure. Now I've these people bitching, and they want him removed, to have a regular recruitment process."

"That's ridiculous. Scott's the right person for the job, and he's popular with the people working for him."

"There's something else. Because of what you did, there are some calls to have you reprimanded or disciplined. You've really caused me a load of trouble."

I'd hoped to apologize and get through it, but it had become more serious than I expected.

"Okay. Damage limitation then. What can we do? And preferably not take the job from him. Can I say there are some special circumstances?"

He laughed. "You're unbelievable. Okay, let's think. Is he a minority, or disabled, or something else that we can say is special?"

"I suppose not. He's an average sort of guy, and perfectly fit. Good-looking too."

"I know that. That's why he's so popular with the women that work around him."

"What do you mean?"

"Well, I know for a fact that he had an affair with one of them. And from what I've heard, she may not be the only one. He's like a stud with that group."

I kept my appearance calm. But I was fuming.

"Do you know, I hate to admit it, but maybe I have taken a bad decision, even though it was in the best interests of the organization. I think the only way out of this mess is to take him back to being acting manager, and have a full recruitment process. And for my part, I'll put out an email to all those involved that due to a misunderstanding, I've inadvertently not followed procedure. Would that work? Without any formal discipline against me?"

He stood up, and came round the desk to me. "I'm sure that would resolve things."

I lowered my eyelids, to look suitably remorseful, then looked up at him.

He's an old man. But rugged and still attractive.

"I feel so stupid, having given you these problems. And I really am sorry. Is there some way I could make it up to you? Maybe I could take you to lunch?"

"You play golf, don't you?"

"I sure do. But I'm not very good."

He smiled. "Neither am I. We'll play sometime, and you can buy me lunch at the club."

I stood up, and kissed him on the cheek. "It sounds perfect."

# 48

As usual, on Friday evening, April was working late, but this time it suited me.

Robin and I were planning what I had to do next day in detail, like a secret military mission. I wanted him to come with me, but he was so sure he'd get found out, and be in trouble with Dawn, that he refused. So I'd be going down on my own.

When April came back, she was tired and went straight to bed. So I watched some TV, and then about midnight, I was ready for bed.

That's when the call came.

It was April's mother, and she sounded hysterical. Reckoned there was a rat in her bedroom. I told her it was probably a mouse, but I couldn't shut her up.

That woke April, and she intervened, trying to calm her mother down. By the end of the call, she was stressed out too. Mother had tried phoning Ben, but he wasn't answering, so it was down to me.

It was pointless protesting. I looked in the store cupboard, and found a piece of two by two timber. Whether it would be any good for killing rats, I didn't know, but it felt solid enough.

When I arrived, she opened the door for me, barefoot and in a nightie. Her face looked red from crying.

"Come in, Grant. Come and get rid of the thing."

I took my jacket off, and went upstairs with her. The bedroom was old-fashioned. Lots of satin and old furniture. She was pointing at a cupboard. "I think it went behind there."

I approached nervously. I wanted to get the thing before it jumped out and bit me. But I heard nothing. I nudged the cupboard. Nothing. So I pulled it away from the wall. With growing confidence, I checked the other furniture.

"Are you sure there was a rat?"

She looked despondent. "I'm sure of it. It must have escaped."

She came close. Very close. "Oh, Grant, I was so frightened."

There were tears forming. What else could I do? I put my arms around her, and she snuggled against me. I ran my hands down her back, feeling the satin of her nightie, smooth against her skin.

I said. "There's nothing here now. You'll be fine."

She looked up at me. Her eyes were wide open, and hopeful.

It was instinctive. I kissed her. Then I realized what I'd done, and pulled away. "I'm sorry. I didn't mean to do that. Please forgive me."

"There's nothing to forgive. It's nice to have a man hold me. A man like you."

She went and turned the lights down, and came back close to me, putting her arms around my neck, and pulling me downwards to her. Then she kissed me, long and passionately.

I said, "We shouldn't …"

She started undoing my shirt, and I didn't stop her, even when she opened it up and ran her hands over my chest.

She was more beautiful than ever in the subdued light. And as delicate as April. I kissed her as softly as I could.

She said, "Oh, I wish I were younger, and you were single. I'd want you to make love to me."

I ran my fingers over her breasts. "And I'd want that too."

She giggled. "It would probably be a disaster. I've not had sex in years. I'd be like some silly virgin."

I didn't know what to say. This woman was asking for it, and I could have her. But what would be the consequences? I couldn't make the next move. I knew it would be wrong.

She kissed me again. "You'd better go now, before I forget you're married."

When I got home, April had gone to bed, but for once I was happy to be on my own. I had a lot to think about. April's mother was quite a woman. I didn't feel guilty, either, about the kiss and the embrace. Maybe I should have, but with what April gets up to, it all seemed fair. I wished now that I had made love to her. That moment wouldn't happen again. And even if it did, she might be satisfied with the kissing and cuddling, without wanting more.

I fell asleep after a while, but then woke up in the early hours from a strange dream, where April and her mother were mixed up, and I didn't know which one was which. After that I slept soundly.

Early next morning, April left for her weekend away with Dawn, in San Francisco. Once she'd gone, I got in my car and headed south.

Microfilm readers are the worst thing imaginable. I'd never used one before, and the library staff explained it all as if I was a five-year-old. Robin would have known what to do, without all that. And he'd have done the job in half the time.

The first step in my plan was to find the article that we'd seen summarized on the web. And that didn't take long, using the index location. I read through it on the screen, and printed it. He had been found dead in his bed, with knife wounds. There was a police comment that it was a frenzied attack, but that was about all they said, at least to the press.

Next I wanted to see if there were any follow-ups.

I got one of the staff, a young girl, to help me. It was tedious, winding page after page in the viewer, both of us looking out for something that matched. Then putting on the next roll of film, and starting again.

I'd almost given up. I'd got to two months after the murder, without anything, then the girl noticed one small news article.

The police had closed their inquiries. They'd got the knife, and there were smudged prints from the killer, but they hadn't got anywhere tracking it further. No mention of DNA, but maybe they didn't do that stuff back then. They'd wanted to contact relatives, but weren't even sure he had any. The article gave the name of the detective. It was one of his last cases, and he was soon to be retiring.

I headed home.

I'd phoned Robin from the car, that I had news, and he was ready for me at his place, with a cold beer and a cooked meal too. He fussed around me, making sure I was okay with the food, but I knew he was keen to see the information. I got out the printouts, and ate while he went through them, line by line.

"It's certainly interesting, Grant. But was there nothing else?"

"Nothing. I went on another three months after that last one, and then I gave up. My eyes were killing me from looking into that viewer."

"That detective probably knew a lot more than it said in the papers. But it wouldn't be sensible to go and ask him. It might open things up, and then next thing they'd know about Dawn and the others, and we'd be in big trouble."

"So it's a dead end?"

Robin frowned. "I wonder?"

He went to his laptop and typed something in. "Aha! I did a search on the name of that detective, and I've got something. He's self-published his memoirs. And we can download it as an e-book."

Robin opened up the memoirs on screen, and we flipped through, page by page, until we found it.

The detective had initially suspected a young man staying at the motel, as he matched a description of someone seen near the dead man's house. But another man staying at the motel gave him an alibi. So the police got some contact details, and left it at that. It was a week later that the police tried to contact them to answer more questions, but found the contact details were false. The detective thought then that it could be these two men that had committed the murder. He would have pursued it, but he was retiring, and there was no photograph to go on. So the case was closed.

Robin looked up from the screen. "It's sad for their father, isn't it. His marriage splits up, and he has some sort of life afterwards, but no contact with his family here. And then he's murdered. I don't think we ever want to tell the women about this."

"I agree. Let's shred these printouts, and forget it."

# 49

*~ ~ ~ ~ April ~ ~ ~ ~*

We'd left behind clouds and rain in Portland, but in San Francisco the sun was shining. The hotel was near the waterfront, and our room was light and airy, with an enormous bed, big enough for three. We'd soon unpacked, and were down at Pier 39, for a walk around the shops and stalls. We'd got to the far end of the pier, and stopped to look at the water below.

Dawn took hold of my arm. "My weekend starts here, then, April. Are you ready?"

I didn't know what she was going to do, but it was bound to be something dramatic. I looked around. Lots of people, but no one I recognized. And not likely to. "Yes, I'm ready."

She put her arms around me, and kissed me. I could feel people watching, but I couldn't do anything. After all, I'd promised.

When she came away from me, her lipstick was smudged, and I started laughing. She didn't know why, but she joined in, and hugged me.

"April, we're going to have a lovely weekend. As lovers."

I looked around, but any interest in us had disappeared. We walked for miles, arm in arm, and every now and then Dawn wanted a kiss. Eventually, we were back at the Pier, and went into a cafe, to eat.

Dawn said, "I felt carefree walking along with you. No thoughts of Robin or Portland. It's been the nicest afternoon."

"Me too. I've had some stress at the office lately, but this seems so far away. And the men can wait. I love being with you."

I leaned across, and whispered, "And not as your sister. As your lover."

Dawn smiled. "I've a mind to come over your side and kiss you now, my darling. What do —"

The food order arrived, and we both sat smirking, while the dishes were laid out.

I laughed. "Let's eat first. Then you can come and kiss me."


In the morning, we had a room-service breakfast, and luxuriated in the big bed, watching the morning news on TV.

"Dawn, what are we doing today? Walking round again?"

"I've something special in mind. Have you heard of the Castro district?"

"No, what's it like?"

"Oh, it's a nice area to walk in, with lots of bars and cafes. We'll get dressed, and head up there. You'll see."

By the time we got back to the hotel in the evening, I was exhausted. Where Dawn had taken me, everyone seemed to be gay, and in our weekend roles, we fitted in perfectly. But walking, drinking, eating, and even a little dancing, and I was worn out.

We sat on a sofa together, looking out of the window. Not a great view, but glimpses of the waterfront.

Dawn said, "Was that a good day, my darling?"

I kissed her. "It was lovely. You know how to treat a girl. But I'm exhausted, aren't you?"

"Not really. But let's get room service, and we can finish the day in bed, just as we started it. And then we can make love again."

"I won't be able to be so active tonight, Dawn. It isn't that I don't want to, but I'm tired."

"Maybe I'll do a striptease to get you in the mood, like that man at your bachelor night."

"That was fun. I wouldn't mind seeing him perform again, would you?"

Dawn looked thoughtful. "Now if you could get Grant to do it, that would be even better. He's well-endowed, better than the stripper."

"But there wouldn't be the atmosphere, with just two of us watching. And we can hardly recruit people."

Dawn laughed. "We've got Robin. We could dress him up as a woman, then there'd be three of us. He'd probably enjoy that anyway. But could you get Grant to do it?"

"I'll see what I can do. And Dawn, my darling, I do love you."

She hugged me tight.

I felt so comfortable, with her holding me.

"Dawn, do you think we're lesbians?"

She laughed. "You do say the funniest things. Of course we're lesbians. But only for the weekend."

"But you like sleeping with me any time, don't you?"

"I love it. But I enjoy sleeping with men too."

"I do as well. I don't know which I prefer."

"That's the fun of it. You don't have to choose. You can have it both ways."

# 50

It was early in the evening. April had been chattering on again about San Francisco, and all the sights, but I made the mistake of yawning, and that made her moody. So we settled down to watch TV, always a good way of letting things calm down. At the end of the program, she switched it off.

"Grant, when I had my bachelor night, there was a stripper there."

"Yes, so what?"

"I was talking with Dawn at the weekend. And we had an idea. What if you were to do a striptease for us?"

I laughed. "You and Dawn come up with some crazy ideas. If you want to hire a stripper, don't let me stop you. But not me, thank you. I'm no stripper, and I don't want to look stupid."

"You wouldn't look stupid. You've the right physique, and I could shave your body first, and rub some oil —"

"No, I don't want to do it. You and Dawn would end up making fun of me."

"We wouldn't. We both think a lot of you. But we liked that striptease, and we'd rather it was you getting close to us, than some stranger. Please say you'll do it. Please, Grant?"

"I'll have to think about it. How far would I strip?"

"All the way."

I was beginning to see the positive side of this. If the girls got drunk, I could have some fun with both of them.

"Do I have to be shaved?"

"Yes, all over, and oiled. So your skin is smooth and shiny."

"Well, maybe. But I want to think about it."

"Grant, darling. If you do it, I know I'll be in the mood for anything afterwards."

185

# 51

Robin looked embarrassed. Dawn said he'd agreed to do it without any real objection, but he didn't look so happy now, standing there in front of us in his briefs.

Dawn said, "I think you need pantyhose first, Robin."

Dawn pulled out a stack of underwear, and found a shade she liked.

Then we watched Robin putting it on. It was quite erotic, almost a striptease, but in reverse. He managed fine, and stood up.

I said, "You've got better legs than me. So Dawn, what next?"

"A bra?"

Robin laughed. "I hardly need that."

Dawn ignored him, and got out a padded bra. "It'll give you a better shape. You want to look good for Grant, don't you?"

She held out a dress. "And I've picked this out for you. I think it'll fit."

He struggled into it, and it was far too tight, but he was already looking feminine.

Dawn sat him down and put some strappy high heels onto him. "They don't really fit, but they'll look fine. Just don't try walking far."

I said, "Just the makeup and the wig, and then you'll be one of us."

We sat him down at the dressing table, with the cosmetics in front of him. He was smiling now, looking in the mirror.

I spent ages on his makeup, longer than I'd spend on my own. And he sat there so patiently while I did it.

186

Meantime Dawn was deciding what jewelry he should wear, trying out necklaces and bracelets until she was satisfied.

Then I got the wig out. My dominatrix wig, with long black hair. I fitted it on him, and smoothed the loose hairs.

Finally we stood him in front of the wall mirror. It wasn't Robin at all now. Any stranger would swear it was a woman, and an attractive one at that. Robin couldn't stop smiling.

The three of us went into the living room, and sat on the sofa, with Robin in the middle. The lights were low, and Grant was waiting in the other bedroom, shaved and oiled, and ready to undress for us. It was exciting, like my bachelor night.

And by now Grant would have hopefully drunk enough to be cooperative.


~ ~ ~ ~ *Grant* ~ ~ ~ ~


They took a long time to get ready. It had been tense to start with, sitting in the bedroom waiting, but I'd filled the time with some very large bourbons, and by the time they called me, I was pretty well relaxed.

So it was time for my show. April had promised she was going to make it worthwhile later on, so now I wanted to get on with it.

When I entered the room, my first reaction was that there were three women there, rather than two. I don't like surprises, but this woman looked cute, until I realized it was Robin.

"Hey, April, this was for you and Dawn. But there's no way I'll do it in front of Robin."

"But he looks like a woman. So what difference does it make, stripping for three rather than two."

I laughed. "That's stupid. How you can think it makes no difference?"

April stood up, and beckoned me to follow to the bedroom.

187

She closed the door. "How dare you call me stupid, and in front of the others too."

"Well, it is stupid. How could anyone think that dressing Robin up will make him the same as a woman?"

"Well, you'll have to pretend. That's not difficult is it? Or are you too stupid to do that?"

"This isn't getting us anywhere. I'm staying in here, and you three can play your games together."

There were tears in her eyes, but then her mood changed. "Are you refusing to do what I ask?"

Her tone of voice made me nervous. "Be reasonable — "

"Because if I thought you were refusing, then I might call Ben, to see what he thinks. Then you could tell him he's stupid too."

Suddenly the evening had changed. It was supposed to be a show from me, and maybe a bit of fun with the two of them, and then a reward from April. But now she was threatening me with that lunatic.

The drink didn't help, as I couldn't concentrate enough for an argument. Not that it would have done any good. Maybe if I kept thinking of Robin as female, it wouldn't be so bad. And a lot better than facing her brother.

"I'm sorry for saying you were stupid. There's no need to call him."

"Then you'll strip for us girls? All three of us?"

I stood in front of them. I still wanted to argue my way out, but it was too late. They were applauding me. All three of them.

April said, "I'll start the music and then you can carry on. We want to recreate my bachelor night, so this time, we're to imagine that Robin is the bride getting married tomorrow, and this is her night."

She put the music on, and I started off with little movements, then one by one removing clothes, and throwing them to the side.

Each time I took something off, they applauded, none more so than Robin. It wasn't that difficult to put out of my mind that he's a man. After all he looked like a woman, and if he was willing to dress up, then why not treat him as a woman?

So I carried on, with that in my mind.

Then I was down to my thong, and I hesitated. But they were waiting, so I took it off, and stood there, to their applause.

April said, "Now stand in front of the bride. Remember this is her last night of freedom, so let's make it special."

I went in front of Robin. It hardened and I couldn't stop it.

Dawn said to him, "Touch it, go on."

Robin looked up at me, scared, and questioning.

I wouldn't want any man to touch me. But April was staring hard, and I didn't want another of her threats. I looked down.

Maybe it was the drink, but Robin didn't seem to be a man anyway now. With the black wig and the dress and the makeup, this looked like a woman, and was behaving as a woman. It was as if Robin had become one of them.

What the hell. I put my hands on my hips, and looked straight ahead. The music had stopped and there was silence in the room.

I said, "Yes, it's okay."

His fingers touched, and then moved delicately over the skin, and I felt it going fully erect.

April clapped her hands with pleasure. "All right, Grant, you can step back now, and take a bow."

All three applauded me. The situation was crazy, but it felt exciting to be standing there naked, with what anyone would say were three good-looking women showing their appreciation.

I bowed to the applause.

# Part 10 – STRANGE RELATIONSHIPS

# 52

~ ~ ~ ~ *April* ~ ~ ~ ~

This time the family gathering was at my aunt's house in the hills. I prefer not to go there, as it's not that clean, and she lets the dogs walk over the chairs and sofas, so the whole place smells of them. She has those plug-in perfume things everywhere to cover it up, and for everyone but me it seems to work. Maybe I'm over-sensitive.

Grant's never keen on these events, but this time he's happy enough. That's because he knows we'll be sleeping together. We've not had sex for two weeks now, and he's desperate. It is unfair on him, but I have fun getting him worked up that way. It makes him very attentive, and careful not to upset me and spoil his chances.

Most of us are staying the night. There are some guest rooms, and two families have brought trailers, but Grant and I will be in a cabin, about a hundred yards from the house. It's actually cleaner than the rooms in the house, but there are always some nasty bugs to get rid of. At least I'm better off than Dawn. Robin is ill, so she's come with mother. Dawn's to sleep on a sofa, and it stinks of dogs.

Grant and I parked the car, and went into the house.

In the living room, Dawn came over to me. "Thank goodness you're here. I'm bored stiff. I'm beginning to think I've nothing in common with some of our cousins, what with all their little brats."

I turned to Grant. "We'd have been here sooner, but Grant took longer than usual to get ready. I'm sure he's beginning to look forward to these events."

Grant laughed. "I wouldn't say that, but I am getting used to them. Now did you want me to check out the cabin for wildlife?"

"Oh, darling, if you could? It was ants and spiders last time I stayed there, and I hate them."

Frank had drifted over. "I'll help, if that's okay?"

Grant nodded agreement, and off they went, chatting about bugs.

Dawn shook her head. "Grant's very forgiving, after what Frank did to him."

"He doesn't blame Frank. He knows he's weak-willed and that it was Ben who was responsible for it all. But even so, he doesn't talk that badly about Ben now. It's funny really."

Mother came over to join us. "What are you two plotting? You're always up to something."

"Oh, we were talking about Grant. He seems to have settled into the family now, doesn't he?"

"Well, I'm all for him. He fixed my air conditioner, and chased away that horrible rat. And I know it's not easy, joining a new family. You've got a good man there, April."

"Did the rat ever come back?"

"No, thank goodness. But if he does, it'll be Grant I call."

"So how are you now? You had migraine last time I spoke to you."

"The doctor's put me on some painkillers, and that seems to be helping. But I'm still not a hundred percent. I was in two minds whether to come."

One good thing about being at my aunt's was that she had so much outside space. The children had room to run around, and be out of the way, and it was a great setting for a barbecue. By about seven, it started getting cool, and we went indoors. Time for winding down, and for a few drinks, before bed.

But mother was looking exhausted.

I went over to her. "Have you got a headache again?"

"A little. I think it's all the chatter. If only this place wasn't so cold at night. I'd much rather be home in my own bed."

"So would I. But we can't all leave. Your sister wouldn't understand."

Dawn joined us, catching the tail end of the conversation.

"Do you want to go home? I don't mind taking you."

"No, I'll stay. We can't have two of us disappearing off."

I said, "How about Grant? He could take you back. He won't be missed."

"But he seems to be happy here. He and Ben even seem to be getting on. No, it wouldn't be fair on him."

"He won't mind, honestly."

Dawn said, "Then I can stay with April at the cabin, instead of on that filthy sofa."

Mother said, "I really would like to go home, April, but —"

I interrupted her, "Then it's settled. I'll go and tell Grant."

The evening wasn't bad, with Dawn in a much better mood. The kids had gone off to their bedrooms, and we'd all had a few drinks, and been pretty sociable. Then we split up, and Dawn and I headed to the cabin.

In the dark, using flashlights, it was creepy, and I wouldn't have gone on my own. But inside the cabin it was nice and cozy. Grant had checked for bugs, and cleared a few dead roaches, and he'd put the electric heater on for us.

Dawn said, "Grant will have got her back by now, won't he?"

"I suppose so. She'll be okay now she's home, with some peace and quiet."

"Grant's probably pleased to be back home too."

"I'm not sure. He was disappointed to have to go back. He had high expectations of tonight. We haven't had sex for ages."

Dawn came close, and put her arms around me. "You poor thing. We'll have to do something about that."

"Dawn, you're awful. Is that all you ever think about?"

"No, but when the situation presents itself, what else am I to think?"

"Well, I don't know if I'm in the mood. I'm tired from all the traveling and the socializing. Let's just go to bed."

She pouted. "But you'd been intending to have sex with Grant, so you couldn't be too tired for that."

I was too weary to argue with her. In any case, whatever was said now, she wasn't going to leave me alone, once we were in bed.


~ ~ ~ ~ *Grant* ~ ~ ~ ~


I'd been looking forward to this family gathering. Instead of us all being stuck inside, we'd have time outdoors, with a barbecue. And it worked out pretty well. I even shared a beer with Ben and Frank. Ben's a strange person, but there are times when I can get along with him. I really wanted to know more about his father, and I tried asking in different ways. But he insisted he knew nothing, and was happy that way. I asked Frank too, but he really did know nothing. So much for that line of inquiry.

We'd gone back into the house for the evening when April came and told me that I'd have to take her mother back. I was pissed off, missing out on our night together in the cabin. But there was no one else, and these days I feel quite protective of her mother.

On the way back, we didn't talk much, as she still had a headache, but by the time we arrived, she was in a better mood.

"Come in for a coffee, Grant, or something stronger if you prefer. I've got whiskey."

"I'll have both if that's okay. Coffee and a whiskey sounds perfect."

She poured me a whiskey that was large enough to knock me out, and went off to the kitchen. I sipped at it, then wandered after her to watch while she made the coffee.

I said, "Can I ask you a question? But it's kind of personal."

"Fire away, I won't mind."

"Why do you wear such dark clothes? It makes you look older than you are."

"I haven't really thought about it. After my husband left, I drifted, and wasn't that interested in what I wore. Now I suppose it's a habit. At work, I'm expected to wear a business suit, and at home the family's used to me like this. But does it really make me look older?"

"You're an attractive woman, and I know you could look younger. I'd say it adds ten years the way you dress and have your hair tied up."

She frowned.

Then I felt guilty. "I'm sorry, I shouldn't have said anything. You look fine as you are."

"But I think you've a point. So if you finish making the coffee, I'll change into something you might approve of."

In her living room, I sat sipping coffee, and working my way through my whiskey. Lovely stuff, five years old. She was a half-hour before she came back, but it was worth the wait. A short red dress, and red high heels, with her hair down, and impeccable makeup. Her lipstick was bright red to match. I'd never noticed before that her lips were just like April's.

She swiveled round in front of me, like a fashion model. "I haven't worn this for years. Do you approve of me now?"

I tried to speak, but choked on the whiskey. I started coughing and couldn't stop, so she came and sat next to me, and patted me on the back, until I'd recovered.

She looked at me. "I take it that's a yes?"

Close up, there were some tiny wrinkles next to her eyes and above her lips, but otherwise her face was flawless. Pale clear skin, set against her long dark hair. And a hint of perfume.

"I don't know what to say. You're beautiful. You're the most beautiful woman I've ever met. I can't see how you can be unattached."

"Oh, I was young enough to remarry, when we split up, but I had four young children, with Frank just a baby. I was too busy with all that, and anyway, not many men would want a load of children as part of the deal."

Then a puzzled expression. "Do you really think I'm that beautiful? What about April?"

"April is the prettiest girl in the world, but she's not as much a woman as you."

Then I kissed her.

She didn't respond. But she didn't object either.

She took her coffee, and sipped it. "You've drunk all your whiskey. Do you want another one?"

"I'd better not. If the police get me on the way home, I'd be over the limit. In fact, I'm probably over it now."

She stood up and brought the bottle over, and poured me another. "Then what's the difference?"

I sipped a little more.

I said, "What should I call you? I can hardly call you mother, when we're together like this."

"Call me Karen. It's my middle name. I'd like you to use it. Just you."

"All right, Karen."

She went across the room, to face a mirror, and swiveled round again. "Do you think my legs are too muscular?"

"No, they're fine. A perfect shape. Why do you ask?"

"It's my job. I'm forever walking around, and going up and down stairs. It keeps me fit, but I think my legs aren't right with this dress."

"They look pretty good from here."

"Then come and look closer. And be honest with me."

I wanted to do more than look, and she knew that.

I went over to her, and leaning down, put my hand on her calf, feeling the shape. She didn't say a word. So I moved my hand up, past her knees to her thighs, under the edge of her dress. I wanted this woman, and I knew she wanted me.

I stood up and put my hands on her shoulders. "Right now, Karen, I wish I was your lover, not your son-in-law."

She smiled. "Be careful what you wish for. Wishes sometimes come true."

I kissed her, and whispered, "Karen, I want you."

"Then kiss me, Grant, this time as my lover."

I put my hands at her neck, and stroked her hair, then pulled her close, and kissed her. For a long time.

I whispered, "I'm going to watch you undress, then I'm going to make love to you. I want us to be lovers all through the night."

"Then can you tell me you love me? Even if you don't really mean it?"

"You're a beautiful and desirable woman, Karen, and … I love you."

I'd said those three words automatically, but I didn't feel uncomfortable or false when I said them.

She was looking up at me, eyes glistening with tears, and I kissed her again.

I do love April, but at that moment, this woman was all I could think of. I wanted to hold her, touch her, kiss her and make love to her.

It was crazy. This was April's mother.

"Karen, I really do love you."

# 53

Dawn had been pestering me ever since the night in the cabin about moving in with me. I'd told her no, and to stop asking, but she kept on and on regardless. It's fun sleeping with her once in a while, and I wouldn't mind trying it for a longer period. But I am married to Grant, after all.

But last night I was furious with him. It was Friday evening and I'd let him sleep with me. We'd made love, and then we'd both gone to sleep.

It was in the middle of the night that he woke me, talking in his sleep. I couldn't make out most of it, but he was writhing around in the bed, and I was having to keep clear of him. Then I heard something odd. He was mumbling, so it was hard to work out, but he said it several times.

It sounded like "Carrie, I love you."

That made my mind up for me. First thing, in the morning, I called Dawn, and told her I was ready to try it for a month. She said she'd start packing straight away.

Then I had Grant to tell, and there was no easy way. But he deserved it.

At breakfast, I said, "Grant darling, there's something I need to tell you. Dawn's moving in with me here for a month. And you'll be staying with Robin."

He stopped mid-bite on his toast. "What's brought that on?"

"It'll be fun for me and Dawn, and you and Robin can get to know each other better."

"I know Robin well enough, what's there to learn?"

"Well, you'll be sleeping with him. That'll be something new."

"What? In the same bed?"

"How else would you sleep there? They've only the one bedroom."

"Hey, that's too much. I don't want to do it."

He looked despondent. But I didn't feel sorry for him, after what I'd heard him say last night. And anyway, I was getting excited now about the whole thing.

I smiled at him. "I'll help get your clothes together. We'll swap around this morning."

"I still think it's unfair. You and Dawn always want to sleep together —"

"Maybe after a few days, you'll be happy sharing a bed with Robin."

He grunted.

I said, "Oh, by the way, who's Carrie?"

"I don't know, why do you ask?"

He looked confused. Genuinely confused. Maybe I'd misjudged him.

"You talk in your sleep. It almost sounded like 'Carrie, I love you.'"

"You can't have heard me right. I don't know a Carrie."

But he'd hesitated too long before he replied, and his face flushed slightly when he said it. So he was hiding something. Maybe Carrie was someone he worked with, and had fantasized about. But who knows whether he had gone further, or was planning to?

"That's funny, as I'm sure that's what you said. Anyway, let's get you packed. Dawn will be here soon."

While we were getting his clothes and belongings together, he kept on complaining, especially having to sleep with Robin. I'd told him it was only for a month, so I didn't know why he had to make such a fuss. I wouldn't let him pack any pajamas, either, and that got us into a real argument. But he never sleeps in them normally, and I told him he was behaving like an adolescent. He'd have argued more if he'd known that Robin always slept naked.

Then Dawn arrived with her suitcase, and off he went, leaving Dawn and me together in the apartment. It was a relief when he'd gone.

She hugged me. "It's going to be as if we're on vacation again."

"Grant was really awkward, especially about sleeping with Robin. Was he annoyed too?"

"He protested a little, but that's all. I've a suspicion he quite likes the idea, although he would never say so."

"Anyway, we can forget them for now. So what are we going to do today?"

Dawn smiled. "We can make love. Or play some games?"

"Dawn, you're a bad girl. We've all day and evening before we go to bed. And then I might not be in the mood. I might want to sleep. We've a month together you know, so there's no need to rush things."

"All right. Let's go to the coast, and find a quiet beach, where we can walk and hold hands, just as we did in San Francisco. How does that sound?"

"It's a lovely idea. And take a picnic?"

"Why not? Then when we're back, let's dress up for dinner, and make ourselves look lovely and desirable. We're always doing it for men, so why not for each other? I'll wear that sheer pink blouse. If I don't wear a bra, you'll see right through it. Maybe that'll get you into the mood."

"Pink's nice. I'll wear pink too. That mini-dress with the low neckline."

"We shouldn't bother with cooking tonight. We'll use the time to get ready, and order pizza."

I gave Dawn a hug, and a kiss. "It's going to be such fun. What do you think the boys are doing right now?"

"I'll find out from Robin what went on, but I imagine they're grumbling about the arrangements."

"Dawn, seriously, if they made the effort, I think they could really bond with each other."

"You don't mean they could get intimate?"

"Heavens, no. Grant wouldn't do that. It was enough trouble getting him to do that striptease."

Dawn looked thoughtful. "He's got too many inhibitions. And that's what's making it difficult. I do have an idea, but I'm not sure you'll approve."


~ ~ ~ ~ *Grant* ~ ~ ~ ~


I put my suitcase down.

"Robin, did you know anything about this before today?"

"Nothing. Dawn got a call this morning from April, and that was it. Next thing she was packing."

"You know we've got to share the bed? Didn't you object?"

"I did. But she argues and argues, and I had to give in. So didn't you object too?"

"Yes, but she wasn't listening. And I know she'll resort to threats if I argue.

"Threats involving Ben?"

"Not just Ben. She scares me too, sometimes, when she's in a bad mood."

I hadn't wanted to go out, but Robin talked me into it. We had lunch at a diner, and then took in an afternoon movie. Back at his place, I settled down to watch the TV, while Robin fussed around in the kitchen, making dinner. I told him to order pizza, but he wouldn't have it, so I let him get on with his cooking.

And dinner was good. He can cook better than April for sure. I'd had one beer, and would have had more of the same, but he'd opened a bottle of Californian red, and we got through that while we ate. It was a good meal, and he's good enough company, but my mind was on the sleeping arrangements.

He cleared the dishes away, and then we watched TV for a while.

At about ten o'clock, he said, "Grant, I'm ready for bed. Are you coming?"

"I'll watch TV for a while, then I'll be along."

But really I didn't want the embarrassment of watching him undress.

When I got to the bedroom, Robin was sitting up reading a book. And as far as I could see, he was naked.

I undressed down to my briefs. He seemed to be concentrating on his book. But something wasn't right.

"Robin, I know it's stupid, but do you mind if I sleep on the right side? It's what I'm used to."

He smiled, and moved across, and I got into the bed.

Robin put down his book, switched off the light, and slid down under the bedclothes.

Finally I relaxed. Maybe this wasn't going to be so bad.

# 54

"Dawn, it's been a week now. We should do something special to celebrate."

"Do you want to go to the beach again?"

"We could do, but shouldn't we do something with the boys? We haven't seen them since we swapped over."

Dawn shrugged. "I don't mind, so long as it's just us in the evening. Maybe we could go up into the hills and do a bit of walking? And perhaps we'll find out how they're getting on together."

"Grant won't say anything, I'm sure of that."

She smiled. "When we're walking, you go with Grant and I'll walk with Robin. I can find out anything from him."

"One thing, Dawn, can we do some cleaning up before we go? The place is beginning to look scruffy."

"Are you saying that's my fault?"

"Well, you don't do much in the way of cleaning, do you? I always seem to be tidying up after you."

She came up to me and kissed me. "You're my lovely little housewife, and I do appreciate it. Honestly, I'll try and make more of an effort. Okay?"

"Well, so long as you do appreciate it."

Up in the hills, it was pleasant to be walking with Grant again. I do love Dawn, but there are times when I'd rather be with him.

"How are you getting on with Robin?"

"I'm managing, but I'd rather be back with you. Does it have to be a month?"

"That's what I agreed with Dawn, and she won't want to change back yet. So is it interesting living with Robin?"

"It's the same as when I was sharing an apartment. We sometimes eat together, and other times do our own thing. He reads a lot, you know."

"But sleeping together, that must be different. You've not slept with a man before. Well, apart from that time in Vegas, and that was only one night."

Grant laughed. "And I don't want to again. I stay on my side, and he stays on his. Is that how you sleep with Dawn?"

Now I had to laugh. "You know darned well it's not like that. We enjoy being close to each other. You ought to try it. Robin won't mind."

It was a good day out, and great exercise. And so nice to be with Grant. When we got to the apartment block, I was almost sad to have to split up again.

Back in the apartment, I said, "So did Robin tell you anything? Grant told me nothing."

"I think that's the way it is. Robin's no good at lying to me, and he said they'd fallen into a pattern of getting along together, like sharing a room at college, with someone who has different interests."

"Well, at least they're getting along with each other, even if they're not that enthusiastic. And I'm enjoying living with you, even as your housewife."

Dawn kissed me. "You're more than that. You're my darling little sister, and for now you're my love interest too. Do you realize that we've three more weeks together?"


~ ~ ~ ~ *Grant* ~ ~ ~ ~


It had been a great day, up in the hills, breathing the mountain air, and walking along with April again. I was hoping that I might get her to finish her little experiment, but she and Dawn are adamant about doing the whole month.

Back at the apartment, Robin and I ate, then started some serious beer drinking. We watched a war movie, and drank some more. Then Robin got out another DVD.

"Hey Robin, not another movie."

He was chuckling. "This one's different. It's only an hour. But first, let's do shots."

"Of what?"

"I've a great tequila, waiting for this opportunity."

The movie was a porno, with a muscular guy having some very graphic sex with two women. The camera got in close. Too close at times, almost a biology lesson. I was drunk enough from the shots, and Robin kept them coming. It was a great evening.

By the time we went to bed, we were both laughing stupidly, as we recalled the scenes from the movie.

I undressed and got into bed, then watched Robin strip off.

"Robin, your skin's very smooth. You've no bodily hair have you?"

"I don't like it, so I shave or wax it."

He slid into bed to lie on his back alongside me, and put the lights out. I put my hand out to feel his chest. It was smooth and soft.

He said, "My legs need doing. I'll wax them tomorrow."

I reached down to his thighs.

"They seem smooth enough to me already."

There was a pause. He said, "Do you like touching my skin?"

I laughed. "I suppose I'm thinking of April. And that porno didn't help."

He rolled onto his side, facing away, laughing too, "I don't mind if you want to pretend I'm April. Go on, try it."

I moved up against his back, putting my left arm under his neck, with his smooth skin against my chest, and his legs against mine. I couldn't resist one more thing for fun. I put my right arm round him, and slid my hand onto his chest. When my fingers touched his nipple, I felt him jump slightly, then relax in my arms.

Then I realized that I had an erection.

It had gone too far, but I froze, not knowing what to do.

I fell asleep like that.

# 55

I put down the phone. "That was intriguing, Dawn. It was the police. Something about an investigation, in the south of the state. And they want to talk to Grant."

"Did they say what it was about?"

"No, he said he had to speak to Grant first. I gave them his cell phone number, but I think I'll go round there and see what it's about."

Robin opened the door nervously, and led me through in silence. Grant was looking pale, so I sat down next to him.

"What on earth's the matter? What did the police want?"

He looked at me, hesitating before he replied. "I've a confession to make. A while back, we discussed finding out more about your father, and you said not to do it."

He looked at Robin, but he looked away, not wanting to be involved.

"I did some research, and found some bad news. I'm afraid he's dead, April."

I wasn't sure what to feel or to say. It's sad when anyone dies. But I never really knew him.

"I wish you hadn't done it, but now you have, perhaps it's just as well. At least I won't wonder any more about him."

Grant coughed, and looked as nervous as Robin. "There's more. He was murdered, about ten years ago."

"Oh, no! That's awful. But how do you know that?"

"There was an old news item on the internet, so then I did a little investigating down there, where it happened. It seems that the police never solved the crime. They didn't know of any relatives, so your family wasn't contacted. I discussed it with Robin, and we decided that it wouldn't do any good to tell you all, and it was best left alone. And that's it. I'm sorry."

I sat back and breathed deeply. "So why are the police in contact?"

"Seems like the library staff told them I'd been looking at the details of his death, so the detective wanted to know my connection to the victim. He asked for names and contact details for your family too. I suppose he'll be phoning them next."

"I hope he's diplomatic when he tells mother. Do you think we should warn them?"

"He told me not to do that. But I don't think he's really interested in the case. He told me he had no choice to re-open it when he got the call from the library, and now he wants to get the information about the family, and get it closed again."

Back in my apartment, I told Dawn all about it. Like me, she was sorry it had happened, but wasn't feeling any emotion about it. She was pleased though that the police would be interviewing her. I don't think she cares who killed him, but she reads lots of detective stories, and she's excited to be part of one.

Dawn said, "Anyway, let's forget all that for now. What about my idea for a show? I mentioned it to the boys, and they're both keen. And they won't be pestering now about swapping back. I told them it would be at least a couple more weeks, and they didn't object at all."

"I wish you hadn't told them yet. I'm still scared at the thought of them watching us. I don't know if I can go through with it."

"But don't you find it exciting? If Grant can strip for us, then surely we can put on something as good for them?"

"It is exciting, but I wish I had more confidence."

Dawn opened her purse, and took out a small glass bottle. "Then this was worth every cent. I got it for Grant,

207

after the trouble we had with him over stripping. But it'll be good for us too. It's called GHB. It'll help us lose our inhibitions."

It was scary to look at it. I've never taken drugs and never wanted to. "Are you sure it's safe?"

"Perfectly. We'll both take some. It'll last an hour or two, and there are definitely no side effects."

"But isn't it some sort of date-rape drug?"

"Not really. It's not roofies, where you forget everything. It's about relaxing and feeling free to do things, that's all."

"It's scary taking drugs. Suppose we take too much?"

"That won't happen. I know what a normal dose is, and we'll only take half."

"All right, let's say it works, and we can do what we planned, without me panicking. But how do you know the men are going to cooperate, with what you want them to do?"

Dawn laughed. "That's easy. We'll give them some too. But they can have a full dose."

"And they'll have no idea?"

"None at all. I'll put it in their drinks."


In the early evening, Grant and Robin came over, and we all watched a movie together. Dawn's choice, with some steamy sex scenes, to get us in the mood. Not that Grant needed it. I know him well enough to see that he was impatient for the main event. Dawn had told them enough to get their interest, and since then Grant's imagination would have been working non-stop.

Near the end of the movie, Dawn refreshed the drinks, giving me a wink.

I was nervous drinking mine, as if it was some magic potion. But I couldn't taste anything. I watched the boys, and they drank without saying a word.

Then the movie finished, and Dawn switched the TV off.

"Now boys, I told you April and I are going to do something different tonight, and that you're going to enjoy it. But you've got your part to play too."

Grant laughed. "I could have guessed. Your ideas usually have a twist."

I said, "Don't worry, it's nothing special. Dawn and I are going to put on a little show for you. You don't have to do anything, other than be a good audience. Well, not much, anyway. Come on."

I led them all into the bedroom. "Clothes off, everybody."

Grant looked suspicious. "Why me and Robin? We're not doing the show."

"That's true, but Dawn and I are nervous enough, and it'll make us feel more relaxed. Now come on, all your clothes off."

Grant shrugged, and he stripped off with the rest of us.

There's a sofa in the room, and Dawn and I had turned it to face the bed, and then put a sheet over it. We both got onto the bed, kneeling, with the men standing watching us. We put our arms around each other and were ready. I wasn't nervous any more, and was feeling excited. It might have been the drug, but I think it was because we were actually doing it, rather than worrying ahead of time.

Dawn said, "You two can sit on the sofa now, and relax."

When they sat down, Grant tried to stay at the edge, away from Robin, but it was futile. The sofa's quite small, and sags, so it was tending to pull them to the middle.

I said, "Grant, get closer to Robin. He won't bite you. And put your arm round his shoulder."

Grant looked confused, but then he did what I said, as if it was nothing unusual. Now that must be the drug.

When they were settled, Dawn said, "Now Robin, squeeze closer to Grant."

Robin said, "I thought we were just an audience."

I replied, "You are, and we're the main act. But we want to get into the mood ourselves, and seeing you two together makes all the difference."

Robin did what he was told. And drug or no drug, I knew he was happy to do it.

Dawn laughed. "Good, now Grant, hold him tight, in case he gets too excited."

I whispered to Dawn, "Not an argument or even one of Grant's looks. That stuff's working. Do you think they're ready for the show?"

"You don't need to ask them. Look at their penises. But I don't feel any different with that drug, do you?"

"Not at all. Maybe it affects men more than women? Anyway, let's get on with it. It's going to be fun."

### ~ ~ ~ ~ *Grant* ~ ~ ~ ~

Anyone looking from outside would have wondered what we were doing. Sitting naked on the sofa, with my arm around Robin, we'd look like a couple of gays. Maybe it was the drink, or watching that movie. Anyway it didn't feel so bad. And it was the first time I'd seen the two girls naked together.

They started their show, and I stopped thinking about Robin.

They kissed each other, and moved around the bed, touching and kissing, while we watched, as if it was a porno movie, right in front of us. Before long, they were stroking each other's breasts, and kissing them too. I love stroking April's breasts, and Dawn's too, but it's even better watching them do it.

The only problem was my penis was getting hard, and beginning to hurt. I'd swear that Robin spent as much time looking at it as he did the girls.

They played around for maybe ten minutes, finishing off with Dawn lying on April, and kissing her, then the two of them rolling around kissing and laughing.

When they were done, Robin and I clapped our appreciation. And my penis got a rest at last.

Then they wanted us out. That was a shame, as I reckoned they might be doing more after we'd gone. But it was late, and I was tired anyway, and ready for some sleep.

Back in Robin's apartment, in bed, both of us naked, with the lights low, I was thinking about what we had seen.

"Robin, that show was pretty good, but how long do you think this is going to continue? It's been four weeks already, and now it's two more. But do they really mean that? Or are they going to keep putting things off?"

"I don't know. But I think the novelty's gone, and it won't be long before we're back to normal. If not in two weeks, it won't be much longer."

"Well, I'm frustrated. I haven't had sex for over a month, and that little show from the girls got me ready for anything."

There was a pause before Robin responded.

"I could give you a massage. I'm really good at it. That would ease your frustration."

I'd never had a massage before, and I wasn't sure I wanted one from a man, but why not? "All right, I'll try it. What do I have to do?"

Robin pushed back the bed clothes. "Lie on your back, close your eyes, and relax."

I stretched out, and he started. Gentle finger pressure on my shoulders, moving around by my neck and then back to my shoulders.

At one point, I opened my eyes, and he put his fingertips lightly to close them. Then I heard him get off the bed, and come back. He put a blindfold on me.

Then he started work on my thighs. The outside, then the inside. He pulled them apart slightly, to go further up my inner thighs.

It was relaxing, and sensuous. Then he moved ever so smoothly to my penis. I tensed up, and my reaction was to stop him, but he was doing it so softly that I relaxed again. I should have been shocked at a man touching me. But tonight I was tired and I didn't care. I'd be happy enough if a woman was doing it, and with the blindfold on, what was the difference anyway? My mind drifted as he worked on it, and I couldn't help smiling.

He whispered, "What are you thinking about?"

"I was visualizing Dawn and April touching each other's breasts. By God, that was erotic."

A few minutes later, I felt a condom going on, and then he continued his massage. It was like a dream. He was lying on top of me now, with one hand on my penis, and the other stroking and squeezing my nipples, just as the girls did in their show. My body was getting hot, and I was shaking slightly. I felt his face against my chest. Then his tongue touching my nipple, and finally his mouth against it, as April had done to Dawn.

I tried to tense up, and stop my body responding.

But it was impossible.

# 56

~ ~ ~ ~ *April* ~ ~ ~ ~

Our two-week extension is up, and we've told the boys that we want a little longer. Grant's furious, but we've told them we're planning a couple of special evenings, and then they can come back to us. That quieted them down. They've assumed it will be like last time, but they're in for a surprise.

Dawn pointed at the screen. "That's perfect. Tight-fitting bodycon. He'll look sexy in that."

"But surely he'd be better in something more feminine. You know, some frills and lace. And a bodycon is going to show his shape is male. We don't want that."

We compromised on a red dress, close-fitting the body, but with lots of loose fabric around the hips. Then a body shaper, and bra, and breast enhancers. And on we went, giggling and laughing as we discussed how he would look. We had the biggest argument over the shoes. Dawn wanted high stiletto heels, but I insisted that he should be able to walk around, without the risk of falling over. For once I got my way, with regular high heels, and a cross-strap to hold them tight.

Dawn sat back. "Well, that's the lot. We've gone to a lot of trouble. So I hope it works. The clothes should be here in a few days, so we can do it next weekend."

"Even if it doesn't go to plan with Grant, it'll be fun dressing Robin up. Like having a doll to play with."

"Maybe I'll prefer Robin that way. But I think Grant'll be all right. Robin told me that Grant has got over his hang-ups about their being in bed together, and they're sleeping closer to each other now. And that's without us doing anything. Once they take the GHB, who knows what we can have them do?"

It was late evening, and I knew the women were planning something. They'd asked Robin to come to them a couple of hours ago, and had told me to wait.

Now I was at their door, and entered.

I first thought that Robin wasn't there, and they had another woman with them. But then I realized that they'd dressed the poor guy up again. This time he was blonde.

He was standing there in a red dress with what seemed a good-sized bust. Pantyhose, high heels, and his fluffy blonde wig. And they'd spent time on the makeup. His face was the color of a peach, with eye shadow, and false eyelashes. And they'd done something with the lipstick to make his lips seem fuller.

"My God, Robin, They've done a real job on you. You look stunning."

He fluttered his eyelids. "The lashes are driving me mad, and they haven't let me look at myself yet."

In the living room, they sat me and Robin on the sofa. Then they brought in the movable mirror from the bedroom and positioned it opposite us, so we could see ourselves. I could see Robin turning his head slightly to check how he looked. He couldn't stop smiling. Dawn brought us all drinks, and then she and April sat down, and she switched on the TV. It was bizarre. The program was a travelogue, of no interest to anyone, but we were all there watching it, with Dawn flitting around, topping up our drinks, and giggling every time she did.

Once in a while, I couldn't help looking across at the mirror. Christ, we looked like a couple.

The program finished, and Dawn switched the TV off, and stood up. April went and switched off the overhead light, leaving only the soft light of the table lamps. They were up to something, but what?

214

"Come over to the mirror, Robin, so you can see yourself properly. You too, Grant."

Robin went and stood in front of the mirror. He kept turning slightly to see from different angles. Then he got up close to see the makeup, and was making little expressions to see how he looked, pouting his lips, and raising his eyebrows.

April said, "Now Grant, admit it. Robin is a woman tonight. An attractive one at that."

I laughed. "I agree. He looks like Marilyn Monroe. And he's even behaving like a woman."

Dawn said, "What do you think of Marilyn's lips? I took ages over them. Do they look kissable?"

"Yes."

April came close. "Then why don't you kiss her?"

"Please, April."

But she stared at me. "Don't you want to come back?"

Her eyes told me that she meant it. Anyway, it was no big deal. And she really did look like Marilyn Monroe.

I went up close, and would you believe it, she looked up at me and closed her droopy eyes for the kiss. Like any woman.

So I took hold of her and kissed her.

It confused me that I could taste vanilla, just as with Dawn, and the kiss lasted longer than I'd planned. When I let go, and stood back, her eyes were sparkling.

Dawn led us back to the sofa. "Can you still see yourselves okay?"

I nodded.

April came and stood in front of us. "You look very romantic sitting together."

"Stop fooling around, April. Can we go back now?"

"All right, you can both go back. It's time you lovebirds went to bed anyway."

Robin said, "Can I change?"

Dawn said, "Not here. Change when you get back. And you'd better take your make-up with you."

When we got back to our apartment, I held the door for Robin. It was only as he walked by, that I realized I'd held all the doors for him. And he was happy enough to go along with it, with a whispered little "thank you".

In the apartment, he stopped to look in the wall mirror.

"Grant, I do look beautiful, don't I?"

"I can't argue with that. They've done a real makeover on you. And it seems to me that you like playing the part too."

"Yes and no. I love the overall effect, but the clothes are tight, and the earrings are hurting my ears."

"Well, take them off. You don't have to keep them on."

"They look nice though, don't they?"

I came closer, and he pulled the blonde hair aside so I could see them better. "They've chosen some expensive stuff for you."

He turned to me. "Before I change back, would you kiss me again?"

"You know I've no choice there, but back here, it's not the same."

"Then forget who I am. Think of me as a woman. And you agreed I was good looking."

The sad glance up at me was that same sloppy look from before, pouting, and with fluttering eyelashes. It was true. Before me was a beautiful woman wanting me to kiss her.

But it wasn't a woman, and I didn't have April threatening me.

"No, Robin. With them, I had to do it, but here I don't. I'm not in the habit of kissing men."

Robin frowned, then stamped off in his heels to the bathroom, and slammed the door behind him.

Then I heard him crying in there. Damn. Now I felt terrible.

I went to the bathroom door, and called him, but he said he wasn't coming out. He'd stopped crying, but was sniffling, which made me feel even worse.

I felt so sorry for him, or was it her?

I called out, "If you want to be Marilyn Monroe for a while, then I'll go along with it."

Marilyn came out. Her makeup had suffered a little from the crying, but it didn't spoil the appearance. Other than making her look more vulnerable.

She whispered, "So you'll kiss me?"

Hell, a woman like this … I'd fuck her if I could.

# 57

It was early evening when we arrived at mother's. She wanted us together, and said there was something she had to tell us about our father. Ben and Frank were already there, with Ben giving Grant an awful look when we walked in.

He approached Grant. "So it's you that's got us into this mess."

"I did nothing wrong. Once I saw that he'd been murdered, it was natural to want to know more. How was I to know the police would follow up on it?"

Ben stormed off and sat in the corner.

Mother was pale. She waited until we were all seated, without a word. She looked at us in turn, then sat down herself.

"You all know by now that your father is dead. I can't feel any grief, as it was so long ago that we lived together, but I'm sorry he's dead, and murdered too."

She took a sip of water.

"There's something you ought to know, that I'll be telling the police. He came up here to visit me ten years ago. From what I understand now, it was only a month before he was murdered."

Dawn said, "Why did he come? I don't remember it."

"He wanted to see me again and to apologize for walking out, all those years back. I said I forgave him. What else could I do? But when he said he wanted to meet you all, and stay in contact with me, I said no. He was disappointed, and gave me all sorts of arguments, until I almost changed my mind. But thank goodness Frank turned up, and it interrupted the conversation. He left shortly afterwards, and I never heard from him again."

Dawn said, "Why weren't the rest of us told?"

"I didn't think it would help any of you to know. So I told Frank to keep it a secret. Maybe that was a mistake, I don't know."

I said, "So what happens next? Are they going to interview us?"

"Yes. They'll be here in a couple of weeks' time. And they're going to take fingerprints and DNA samples."

Ben looked up. "Why are they doing that? Are we suspects?"

Mother shrugged. "He said it was for elimination and was routine. But yes, I suppose we're all suspects. Except for Grant and Robin."


~ ~ ~ ~ *Grant* ~ ~ ~ ~


After we left, the four of us went to get something to eat. At the restaurant, the main topic was of course the police investigation.

April said, "I know it's sad that he died, but I hardly remember him, so I don't feel anything. What about you, Dawn?"

"Same here. And he couldn't have been that nice a person, walking out on mother."

"Oh, I don't know about that. We don't know the background. Maybe he was unable to cope with married life, or something."

I said, "Well, whatever he was like, I wish we hadn't started looking for him, now the police are upsetting you all."

Dawn said, "But who could have done it? And why? They can't suspect us can they? All this about fingerprints and DNA makes us look guilty. And surely it's too late to do anything ten years on?"

"I'm not so sure. If they still have the knife, then they can do forensics on it. Things have moved on in ten years. I'm sure there's no family involvement, but it is an open case, and maybe something will lead the police in a new direction. And after all, it's quite a coincidence that he visited here before his death. The police are bound to be thinking about that."

"You're right. Maybe he had some old enemy here, who saw him, and followed him back? Or maybe when he was here in Portland, he got into an argument —"

April interrupted, "I've had enough of this. Can we talk about something else?"

There was a silence, then I said, "Here's a new topic. When are you and I going to be back together?"

"Not long now. We'll have one last show, and then we can all move back. But we have to decide what sort of show."

I smiled. "Maybe you girls can do one of your performances again on the bed? That was pretty good."

Dawn said, "I bet you're only asking that so you can sit with Robin."

That shut me up. We sat in silence, nursing our coffees, then April started giggling like a little kid.

"I've had an idea. Maybe you men should be on the bed next time, with Dawn and me watching you?"

I almost choked on the coffee. "No way."

Robin added, "Grant and I didn't ask to be in this situation, but we're making the best of it. You two seem to want to humiliate us, and it's not fair."

Dawn replied, "It is fair. We performed for you, so you could do the same for us. That's perfectly fair in my eyes."

April was looking directly at me, and I knew what she was thinking. But this was going too far. I'd rather take my chances with her or Ben, if she tries that on me.

# 58

It was going to be an exciting day for me and Dawn. The day of the final show. But Ben's actions were dominating our thoughts.

"But Dawn, he can't have been involved in the murder of his own father, surely? I mean what motive could he have?"

"I don't know. But he didn't want to give the police his fingerprints and DNA, so there must be a reason for that. Perhaps there's something we don't know about. Anyway, they've got the prints from the rest of us, so hopefully that's the end of our involvement."

"I hope the police don't hurt him when they catch him."

Dawn shook her head. "Ben's cunning, and he won't be easy to catch. He'll have already hidden away somewhere. Maybe he's even gone up to Canada. Anyway, let's forget about him, and think of this evening."

I said, "Is everything ready?"

"As ready as it can be. I've joked about the possibilities to Robin, but as soon as I hint at a show from them, he won't talk about it. So we'll definitely need the GHB again."

"I haven't dared mention it to Grant. He thinks that we'll be doing a repeat performance, otherwise I don't think he'd come."

Dawn frowned. "Then they're both going to need more than a regular dose. From what I understand of this stuff, they'll do nearly anything then."

"So if we do get them on the bed, what will we have them do?"

"They'd have to embrace, and kiss. It would be fun to have them do more than that, but I'm not sure they'd do it, even if they're drugged. I wish I knew more about the effect it has, but surely there's got to be a point where they'll resist."

I laughed. "If you mean something homosexual, Grant wouldn't do that, whatever state he was in. But maybe we could get them to French kiss?"

"Then it's an experiment. We'll get them on the bed, and see what we can get them to do."

"Do we need to take some of it too?"

"I don't think so. I think we've lost most of our inhibitions already."


In the evening, we'd all been watching TV, and at about ten o'clock, Dawn brought a last round of drinks. Champagne, to celebrate that tomorrow we'd be swapping back. Of course, the boys were getting more than champagne.

Dawn sidled up and put her arm round me.

"It's show time again, boys. Let's finish off the champagne, and relax a little while, and then we'll get started."

I could see that Grant was impatient to see us performing again. We finished the drinks, and chatted, but I couldn't concentrate. All that was on my mind was whether it had taken effect, and how far Grant would be willing to go.

Dawn stood up, and we followed her into the bedroom.

"Clothes off, everyone."

Not that she needed to say it. Grant had started undressing as soon as he entered the room.

Dawn asked, "How are you feeling, Grant? Ready to sit with Robin?"

Robin was looking at him eagerly.

Grant frowned as if he didn't quite understand. "Yes, I'm ready."

When we were all naked, Dawn sat down on the sofa, and I sat next to her, leaving them standing there in the middle of the bedroom.

I couldn't help giggling. "Tell them, Dawn."

Dawn looked at the two men, as if inspecting them.

"You're both good looking individually, but you're going to look much better sitting together. So, onto the bed, please."

Robin got onto the bed. Grant looked as though he was going to say something, but he got on it too.

Dawn said, "Now we want a show from you this time. What are you going to do for us?"

Grant reacted, "We're not putting on a show like you did. That's ridiculous."

I said, "It wasn't so ridiculous watching us, was it?"

"But that's different. It's what you girls wanted. Robin and I never agreed to do a show."

He ran out of words. There was a silence, then Robin said, "Come on, Grant, I don't mind."

Grant looked at us sitting on the sofa, and then at Robin next to him, and was clearly confused. I felt sorry for him, but after all, he was happy enough for me to do things for him.

I said, "Go on, Grant, he's waiting for you. Get closer."

He moved across the bed, next to Robin.

Dawn squeezed my hand, and whispered, "I'll let you into a secret. I've given them more than a double dose, to be sure. Now let's see how far they'll go."

She looked at them. "Now, both of you lie on your side, facing each other. And then show us how friendly you can be to each other. Nice and friendly."

Neither said a word. They both did as they were told, and Grant even put his arm around Robin, who cuddled up in response. Dawn was gripping my hand tight. She whispered to me, "Now it's your turn to say something."

I said, "Now I want you to do something for me. I want to see you kissing."

223

Grant seemed to be in a daze. He nodded agreement, and then kissed Robin, who responded. It was scary what we could have them do. But would they go to the next step?

I said, "You could do better. Watch me."

They turned towards me. I faced Dawn, and put my tongue out, then gradually moved to kiss her. We carried on for nearly a minute, kissing and with our tongues showing occasionally.

When we came apart, I said, "Now, can you men do it as well as that?"

Robin smiled at Grant. "I think we could do better."

They started kissing again, but this time they used their tongues, and then they seemed to forget about us for a few moments. Grant got so excited, he nearly rolled on top of Robin. It was almost like watching sex.

When they'd come apart, Dawn said, "That was great. Well done boys."

She applauded, and I joined in.

The whole thing was surreal. Grant was doing things he would never do usually, but he was evidently enjoying it.

He said, "What do you want us to do now?"

Dawn looked at me, and whispered instructions.

We got off the sofa, and went to stand next to the bed.

Dawn said, "Robin, hold Grant's penis."

Robin put his hand round it, and it stiffened.

"How would you describe it, Robin?"

He stroked it. "It's beautiful."

Dawn smiled. "Would you like him to put it into you?"

~ ~ ~ ~ *Grant* ~ ~ ~ ~

I'd had mixed feelings about the evening ahead. Watching the girls was great, but having to sit naked with Robin was another matter. Last time, I must have let the drink get to me, so it didn't seem so bad, but not what I'd want anyone to know about. I'd decided to drink less this time, and it seemed to be going well, but then it all changed with the champagne. I'm not used to that stuff, and Dawn gave us plenty.

And then it was like being in a dream. Me and Robin on the bed, with the girls watching, and telling us to do things. Part of me wanted to stop, but I couldn't get round to saying it before they had us doing something else.

But even with the girls watching, it didn't seem so unnatural. Robin's not a woman, but he's as good-looking as some. And he seemed happy enough to be playing the games.

But then Dawn said something to Robin about my penis.

It took me a second to realize what she'd said, but before I could think it through, Robin replied, "Yes. I think I would like that."

Dawn said to him, "Do you know what you're agreeing to?"

He nodded.

She said, "What about you, Grant? He'd love you to push your big penis into him. Won't you do that for him?"

I was confused, and muttered, "I don't know."

Dawn said, "Robin, kneel down, ready for him."

Robin went to the middle of the bed, and got into a kneeling position, with his hands flat down in front of him.

I started to say something, but April interrupted. "Now don't argue. Robin's willing, so you should be too."

I moved behind Robin, with my penis touching the inside of his thighs.

Dawn said, "Look in the wall mirror. You two look so erotic. Beautiful and erotic."

She was right. My body on his, like some classic sculpture. The girls applauded again, then stood up.

Dawn said, "Well done. It was a great show. You can get dressed now, and we'll have a drink waiting for you."

The two girls left, arm in arm, and closed the door.

We didn't move. We were both looking at the reflection.

I said, "It does look erotic doesn't it?"

"Very. You're so muscular, and the way you're holding me, …"

I laughed. "This is all crazy. I'd never have thought I'd do this. It's as if we're a couple of gays about to have sex."

It was less than an hour later that we were back at Robin's apartment, lying in bed in the dark. I couldn't stop thinking about what we'd been doing. And how erotic we looked in the mirror.

Robin said, "I thought they were going to make you do it to me."

"So did I."

Robin sighed. "I've always wondered what it would be like."

"So did you want me to do it?"

"I was confused with what was happening. And I was scared when you were holding me. You're so strong, and I felt trapped. But it was exciting too. If you'd carried on, I couldn't have stopped you."

"Well, I was confused too, …"

In fact, I was still confused. I didn't understand how we could be talking so calmly about having sex together. Maybe that's how men are in prison, where it's the only sex they can get. And no one says they're homosexuals. Maybe that's the situation I could imagine I was in. Locked up in a cell with Robin.

But I was tired, and the champagne was wearing off, so it wasn't what I wanted.

It was bizarre thinking back though, to being on that bed. I was sure the women were going to get me to fuck him.

And I was ready to do it.

# Part 11 – DEATH THREATS

# 59

~ ~ ~ ~ *April* ~ ~ ~ ~

It's been nice having Grant back with me for the last few days. I love Dawn so much, but we both needed a break. And Grant's been so attentive, like when we were first married.

I think he's embarrassed about the show he did for us with Robin, but I can't see why, as it was only a bit of fun. Still, if he doesn't want to talk about it, that's fine by me. Dawn says Robin's the same. They're both finding it difficult to believe that they did it, but we know why they were so cooperative.

It was early evening when mother phoned, sounding tearful. Something about there being a problem, and we had to go to her straightaway. What made it more mysterious was that she said that Grant had to pack some clothes, ready for a trip. And she wouldn't discuss it further on the phone.

When we arrived, she was waiting at the door and ushered us in. Then, without a word, she burst into tears, and sat down. Grant sat next to her and put his arm round her, until she'd calmed. He can be so nice at times.

She looked up. "The police were here to ask me more questions about when your father came back here. They say that Frank and Ben murdered him."

I dropped into a chair. "That's ridiculous. How can they think that?"

"They've exhumed the body, and there's trace evidence on the body itself and on the knife that killed him.

They've already arrested Frank, and they're looking for Ben."

"But it's unbelievable. Why would they have done it?"

"No one's any idea. And Frank's clammed up. That's why they want Ben."

Grant said, "But why did you want me to pack?"

"Ben phoned, not long after the police had left me. He'd heard about Frank, and I told him what the police had said. The thing is, Grant, he blames you, and he says he's going to kill you."

Grant looked at me, then back to her. "Is April safe? And you and Dawn? And what about Robin?"

"It's you he blames. He's crazy. He always has been. You've got to get away."

"I could go to Seattle, and stay with friends, but for how long? If the police don't catch him, I'll be forever watching out for him. And what about my job? I can take a couple of weeks off, but then what?"

I said, "Is there no way we can reason with Ben?"

Mother shook her head, "You were close to him when you were younger, so you'd know him as well as anyone. He'll probably call me again, and I'll try, but I think it'll be a waste of time, don't you?"

"Then what can Grant do?"

She looked at him. "There is one way, but it's risky."

"I'll try anything. What do I have to do?"

She opened a cupboard, and took out a battered cardboard box.

Inside was a revolver with a short barrel, and a box of bullets.

"Grant, I've a cabin up in the woods. It's hardly been used since the children grew up, but it's clean, and there's bedding and canned food. When Ben calls, I'll tell him that you forced me to give you the key."

Grant frowned. "Then he'll come after me. Good, I'll be ready."

I grabbed hold of him. "It's too dangerous. You only know part of what he's like. He's devious and he's crafty, and he knows the area round there. Please don't do it."

Grant picked up the gun. "It's in nice condition."

He pocketed the gun and the ammunition.

"If we don't do this, Ben could come after me any time, anywhere, when I don't expect it. At least this way, I'll be ready and prepared."

# 60

I'd taken some bread and supplies to the cabin, enough for a couple of weeks, as well as some extra ammunition. And once up there, I'd had a little practice with the gun. At short range, I could place a shot within a couple of inches, so I was confident enough about meeting Ben face to face. And then Karen had phoned. Ben was on the move, so from that point, I was on guard, waiting for him.

For the first couple of nights, it had been hard to sleep, but after a week, I was beginning to wonder if he was going to come after all.

Maybe he'd run for it, to another state, or to Canada, and was never coming back. In which case it was pointless sitting here eating canned meat and baked beans every day.

What was even more aggravating was the thought that back home, they were all living normal lives. April seemed to be getting on fine without me, and had Dawn back there in our apartment. When I phoned her yesterday, she was even too busy to talk to me, and I had to phone back.

I'd phoned Robin too. He was sympathetic, but he seemed occupied with his own affairs, and like April, had no more news of Ben.

It was time to collect some wood for the stove.

It ran out yesterday evening, and I'd been wary of going outside to get more, so I had cold food last night. I wasn't going to have that again.

# 61

It was nice having Robin round for dinner. It was funny, but it didn't seem as if he was Dawn's husband, but rather a guest, and we were the couple. He's usually happy enough with the situation, when he's sharing with Grant, but he hates being on his own, and I felt quite sorry for him.

Grant was grumpy too when I told him about Dawn being back, but he ought to try and see my viewpoint. I don't want to be on my own because he is, and having me unhappy wouldn't help him in the slightest.

I said, "Robin, did you enjoy the meal?"

"It was delicious. Did you both do the cooking?"

"Heavens no, Dawn's no good in the kitchen."

Dawn smiled. "I can't be good at everything."

Robin said, "Well, it's nice to be here, and not on my own for once. Even if sometimes you have fun at my expense."

I said, "What do you mean by that?"

"You know, like dressing me up as a woman."

Dawn said, "You didn't mind that at all. In fact, you told me you enjoyed it."

"All right, maybe I did. Maybe that wasn't a good example."

I said, "Would you let us dress you up again? Tonight?"

He flushed, "I don't know."

Dawn jumped up. "That's a lovely idea. I'll go and get the clothes from our apartment. Robin, go to the bathroom and strip off. You're going to be Marilyn again."

Dawn almost ran, in her enthusiasm, and a hesitant Robin went to the bathroom. It was only a few minutes

231

before she returned, and by the time she put the clothes down, Robin was back in the living room, with only his briefs on.

We got him dressed, and then got to work on the makeup.

While I was doing his eye shadow, he said, "Can I do that myself?"

"You'd probably make a mess."

"Then will you show me how to do it?"

So the makeup session turned into a teaching session. Actually, he was quite good at it, and seemed intent on learning what to do. Finally the blonde wig, and he was perfect. Dawn got us all to the large wall mirror, to see ourselves. Robin looked as feminine as Dawn and me.

I said, "If only Grant could see us now. He wouldn't know which of us to go for."

Robin said, "Do you suppose it's wrong to be playing games, when he's there alone, and waiting."

Dawn shook her head. "It's tough out there for him, but he's a tough guy. He wouldn't want us all to be sitting here miserable would he, April?"

"No, he'd want me to be happy, not sad. Now what are we going to do next?"

Dawn said, "Let's go out, all three of us."

Robin exclaimed, "No! I can't do that."

"Yes you can. We'll go out of town and visit a diner, for coffee and pancakes. It'll be the perfect test to see if the waitress can tell you're not a woman."

"But what if she does realize? I'll feel terrible. My voice will give me away."

"Then keep your mouth closed when the waitress is around, and I'll place the orders. But don't forget to smile."

"What if there's someone there who recognizes me? I'll be so embarrassed, I'll —"

Dawn stood up. "Come on, Marilyn. We're going, and no more excuses."

# 62

I was already awake when I heard the noise. I'd propped some nails against the doors and windows, and the sound of them falling to the floor was distinct in the silence.

So this was it. I checked my watch. Exactly three o'clock. I got out of bed, and went to a corner of the room, pressing myself against the walls. And pointing the gun at the bedroom door.

And waited.

But there was no sound. Nothing at all.

Minutes went by, still with no sound.

I'd definitely heard the nails drop, but could it have happened without something being opened? Perhaps too finely balanced, and then a draught?

I lowered the gun, but kept it ready.

I'd give it five more minutes, and then I'd go and look.

But barely a minute had gone by when I heard a slight noise outside the door. I raised the gun again.

And then the door flew open.

A shadowy figure lurched towards the bed, and then hesitated, realizing the bed was empty. He swiveled round, and saw me, then instantly changed direction towards me, with a knife in his right hand.

I fired, and he stopped, but still holding the knife.

I knew already it must be Ben, but now in the dim light I could see it was him. He stared at me, trying to say something.

I suppose I should have said "drop the knife", but I'd had enough of him and his lunatic ways. It had to be brought to an end.

233

This time I aimed carefully at my target, and fired again. He crumpled to the floor.

In the movies, someone always checks a pulse to see if the person is really dead. I didn't need to do that. This is a solid old gun, and I'm a good shot.

I went into the kitchen, and put wood on the stove. I needed a coffee, and then I'd be ready to call the police, and go through their hours of questioning. Knowing the cops, they'll probably try to charge me with unlawful possession of the gun. Or entrapment. Or some other shit charge.

But Ben was dead, and that's what mattered.

# 63

It was early evening when he got back.

"Come in, Grant. You'll have to tell us what happened. The police told us that Ben was dead, but wouldn't say any more than that."

We went through to the living room, where Dawn had poured him a drink.

"There's not a lot to tell. I'd almost given up on him coming. It had been over a week since your mother told him where I was, and to start with I was scared, even to go to sleep. But with no sign of him since her call, I was thinking of locking the place up and coming back home."

"But he did come?"

"I was asleep when he broke in, but I'd heard him. Otherwise I'd be dead now. But even though I was prepared, he was almost too fast for me. He burst into the bedroom with a knife in his hand, and came straight at me. I reacted instinctively, and fired twice. I didn't want to kill him, but there was no choice."

"We've all been so worried about you. I'm glad you're back okay."

"So am I. Now I want to get some quality sleep."

I looked at Dawn, but she avoided my glance.

"The thing is, Grant, I told you on the phone. I've got Dawn staying with me."

He looked confused. "But now I'm back?"

I went over to Dawn and put my arm around her. "For now, Dawn's staying with me. You'll be back with Robin for a while."

235

I was ready for an argument, but fortunately he was tired. He picked up his bag, and walked out. We heard the door slam.

"Oh, Dawn, I feel terrible. After what he's been through, it's not fair on him."

"But what about me? You can't get me here when it suits you, and then cast me aside. That's not fair either."

"But he is my husband, and I'm his wife."

She came close, and kissed me. "While I'm here, I'm your husband. And Grant'll be all right. Let's have a few more days together, until the funeral, and then we'll swap back. And I'm sure Robin will look after him meantime."

### ~ ~ ~ ~ *Grant* ~ ~ ~ ~

Robin opened the door to me, and I had to smile. He was dressed up again as Marilyn Monroe, and looking pretty good in his blonde wig.

"What's with the dress, Robin? It's not one of April's plots is it?"

He smiled. "No, I was fooling around. I know you want to be with April, but I thought if I dressed up, at least I'd take your mind off things for a while."

"Well, I appreciate it. It's a better welcome than I got at April's."

"Go and sit down, Grant. I've got some food prepared. I won't be a minute."

"So you're playing the housewife too. In that case, get me a beer, will you?"

He smiled, and then trotted off in his high heels, like a catwalk model. He was walking in them now without hesitation. Maybe he'd been practicing.

While we ate, he chattered away about what had been happening. He was all excited that the girls had taken him out somewhere, dressed like this, and no one had realized he wasn't a woman.

After that, we watched the news on the TV, sitting separately. Robin means well, but it's not the same. And it hadn't taken my mind off April. She knew I'd want to be back with her, after being away, but Dawn was getting priority over me. Those two would be having their lesbian fun tonight, and I'd be stuck here with Robin.

I looked over at him. He did look feminine, but it was still difficult to see how I'd got so intimate with him previously. The guy's pleasant enough, but not to fool around with. I must have had too much to drink, so one solution tonight might be to get drunk again, and then maybe I'll want to do something. But I needed a woman, and I didn't want to have to get drunk.

I went into the bedroom, closed the door, and made the call. She was a long time answering.

"Karen, can I come over?"

"Grant, it's late. I've already gone to bed."

"So, can I come over?"

There was a pause. "You're not with April then?"

"No, she's got Dawn with her, and I'm having to stay with Robin."

"So that's it. I'm in reserve when you don't have other options?"

"Hell, Karen, I'd be with you any time I could. Please let me come over."

"Are you going to want to make love to me?"

"I've been in that cabin for days, on my own, so what do you think?"

Another pause. "All right. You can come."

# 64

At the funeral, I was in tears. Ben could be awful at times, but he was my brother, and I had some good memories of when we were young. The memories weren't all good, but when someone dies, you try to forget those.

And I felt so sorry for Frank. The police had given him a hard time, with the interrogations, and he'd looked pale when I first visited him. Later on, he didn't look any better physically, but he seemed more relaxed, after he'd made a confession. And not only to his involvement in the murder of our father. He'd told the police how Ben had killed that poor man that worked for me. As it was Ben that had actually committed the murders, with Frank only an accomplice, the police had done some sort of deal, and allowed him to come to the funeral, under escort.

I was told that Ben had killed that ex-employee to protect me. I'd been glad that he was no longer a threat to me, but now I felt guilty, even though it wasn't my fault.

I'd said hello to Frank, but that's all. Grant spent a few minutes with him too, but Dawn wouldn't talk to him. I can't blame her. The police told us that Frank was genuinely confused about what led up to father's death. It had started with Ben telling father not to upset mother again, but then it all got out of hand, and Frank didn't understand why.

At the wake afterwards, Grant said he was sorry that anyone should die, but he couldn't feel too concerned about someone who had been trying to kill him. And we both knew about the times that Ben hurt Grant.

I said, "I know you've never liked Ben, and were angry with him at times, but it's as much my fault as his. If I

238

hadn't told him of my problems, he wouldn't have intervened with you. So I'm sorry if I've been the cause of it all."

"I've long ago forgiven you. And I suppose in a way I partly forgave him too. He was only doing what he felt he had to as a brother. Some might say he went too far for a sister, but maybe there's some aspect of him I don't know about."

I felt myself flush. "Are you thinking of changing things now he's gone?"

"What would I change?"

"Well, at one time you were forever arguing when I asked you to do things. Sometimes it was only when Ben intervened that you agreed to go along with me."

"I don't want anything to change. I love you, April, and I want us to stay together. So if that's what it takes, I'll do what you want, no question, whatever it is. I'll be happy with the way things are, provided you don't move me out permanently to have Dawn with you."

"But once in a while is okay?"

"If that's what you want."

I laughed. "I wonder what else you'll let me do? Maybe I'll need to test you?"

"Test me all you want, but right now I'm going for another beer."

Dawn came over to me. "You're looking cheerful for a funeral."

"I've been talking to Grant. I thought with Ben gone, he might want to change things, but he wants nothing of the sort. And he says he'll still let me make the decisions."

"I'm not sure I believe that. He was scared of Ben. That makes a big difference."

"Maybe, but I know he's a little bit scared of me too."

239

Good riddance.

That's what I was thinking about Ben. But I had to be more diplomatic when talking to the others at the funeral. I've noticed that once people are dead, their bad points are forgotten, and their good points become more important. Not that Ben had many good points.

Frank was there under escort, and I felt sorry for the poor mutt. Ben had more or less told him what to do, but now he was on his own answering the charges. With a hazy memory too, he was perfect material for the prosecution. They'll have him locked up for life, no doubt sharing a cell with another Ben.

I asked the police for a few minutes with him, and they reluctantly agreed, so long as I didn't discuss the cases against him.

"Hi Frank. I'm sorry about what happened with Ben."

"You don't have to be sorry about anything. Ben wasn't nice to you. If it wasn't for him, we'd have been good friends, I know it."

I wasn't so sure about that, but I felt sorry for the poor guy.

"I think you're right. You and I have never disagreed on anything. It's a shame how things worked out. We could almost have been brothers."

Frank leaned closer, "One day, I'll tell you some family secrets."

"Oh yes, what sort of secrets?"

He frowned, as though he was deciding whether to tell me more.

"About Ben. But if I tell you, you mustn't say anything to April."

I nodded agreement, and put on a serious expression for him.

"Frank, I won't tell her a thing. So what's the big story?"

He was nervous, and looked around, as if Ben was still watching him.

"I can't say. You'll have to ask April."

"What though? What do I ask?"

"Ask her how she had a hold over Ben. He did anything she wanted, including the bad things he did to you. But ask her why. And I can tell you it goes back a long way, before you were on the scene."

"So Ben was being coerced?"

Frank laughed. "I wouldn't say that. He liked doing things for her, and he knew he'd be rewarded."

"Now you've got me hooked. What sort of —"

But his police escort interrupted. Frank had to go.

# 65

It was a couple of days after the funeral, and Grant was back with me. It was comforting to know he was lying there next to me, after all that had happened. Dawn's so nice, but with Grant I feel protected, as well as cared for.

In the dark, I said, "Maybe we should have that test tomorrow evening."

There was silence. Then he said, "What sort of test? Is it going to be unpleasant for me?"

"I haven't decided what to do yet, so I don't know. You'll still do a test, won't you? To show me I'm still going to have things my way?"

"I suppose so. But maybe I'll want a reward."

I wasn't sure what he meant, unless it was about having sex.

Then he said, "If I do it, you're to tell me all about Ben."

I felt my body stiffen, and I knew I was breathing faster. He'll have noticed.

"What do you mean, all about Ben?"

"Do I have to spell it out? I've always wondered why Ben was at your beck and call. Now he's gone, I want to know the truth."

We lay there in silence again.

Suddenly the idea of the test seemed stupid. I already knew he'd do whatever I wanted. And if I were going to tell him about Ben, I'd rather get it over with, and do it in the dark.

"Grant, forget the test. It was a silly idea. And I'll tell you about Ben, anyway. But you may not like what you hear. Are you sure you really want to know?"

Grant muttered a yes. Maybe he'd already suspected or guessed something. It was time for the truth.

"I was eleven when he first started, but for all I knew he'd wanted to do it sooner. I'd had a party and everyone had gone. We were upstairs, the four of us, and mother was downstairs watching TV. Dawn suggested we play hide and seek, so she and I and Frank went off and left Ben counting.

"I was in a wardrobe, behind the hanging clothes, when Ben opened the door. I thought he'd call out, but he didn't. He came in too, and pulled the door closed."

"Didn't you think that was odd?"

"I thought it was something to do with the game, playing a trick on the others, so I kept quiet as he moved in next to me. It was cramped in there, with all the coats and now with him, and I was hot, almost suffocating in the darkness. Then I felt his hands on me. He was touching me, but not saying a word. I didn't know what to do."

"Were you frightened?"

"No, not really. But I was surprised. I stayed still while he explored me with his hands. Even over my panties, he was pressing slightly, as if he was feeling the shape of everything. Then we heard Dawn calling, and he jumped away from me, and we both got out of the wardrobe."

"That's terrible, and you were just a kid."

"That was the first time. After that he got braver and started coming to my bed at night."

"Why didn't you tell your mother?"

"I was scared to. I told Dawn, but she laughed about it. He'd done it with her, and she liked the attention."

"And it didn't stop?"

"No, but it wasn't that often. Maybe every two or three months. And after a while I got used to it. But I was fifteen when it went further. It was night, and I felt him creeping into bed with me. But this time was different. He was naked, and he was very excited. He'd probably been planning it for a while, or at least thinking about it. He had sex with me."

"That's awful. You must have felt so helpless."

"Funnily enough I didn't. I knew what he was going to do, and I didn't want it, but I was still interested in the whole process, as if I was someone else observing it. He was unsure at first, and maybe I could have told him to stop, I don't know. But I could tell when he'd gone past that, and it was his instincts driving him. Then I didn't feel helpless at all. I felt superior to him. Me so cool and unemotional, and him not even in control of himself."

"And you still didn't tell your mother?"

"I thought about it, and one day, maybe a week later when we were alone, I told Ben what I was thinking. I've never seen anyone so scared. He started apologizing, and begging me to forgive him, and then he started crying like a baby. So I calmed him down. I said I wasn't angry, and he hadn't hurt me, so I was willing to forgive him. He said he'd do anything for me, I only had to ask. Well, I'd been having trouble with a boy at school, pestering me, so I said I'd forgive Ben completely if he could put a stop to it."

"And I can guess what happened next. The boy got a visit, didn't he?"

"I felt awful. Next day at school, the poor boy had an enormous black eye. He could hardly open it. And far from bothering me, he kept out of my way altogether. And that's how it started. Ben's always been there to protect me, and to do what I ask. As you know."

"But surely you couldn't have that hold over him all these years, for what he did as a teenager?"

I hesitated. "Can't you guess?"

"You mean it went on?"

"He was infatuated with me. Once in a while, I'd let him sleep with me. I didn't particularly enjoy it, but it was so good to have him as a protector."

"Even after we were married?"

"Only once. I'm sorry, Grant."

"And did he sleep with Dawn too?"

Only when we were young. It was me he was keen on. He wasn't at all happy about us getting married. Maybe that's why he was a bit excessive when he punished you."

Grant lay back, and breathed deeply.

I said, "So now you know. Are you angry with me?"

"No, not you. I'm glad you told me, as it explains a lot. But he was a real bastard, starting when you were an eleven-year old."

"But I told you, it didn't really upset me. And he wasn't that old himself at the time. I'm sure I could have stopped it, but I chose not to."

"And does Dawn know all this?"

"A lot of it, but not everything. And she didn't see the harm in it. In fact she was jealous that I was getting the attention, not her."

Grant sighed. "What a family."

"Actually, Grant, there's something else. You might as well know everything. He started getting protective of mother too."

"Hell, you don't mean …?"

"No, nothing like that. But he got over-protective. I know he scared off a couple of men that were interested in her. She never knew."

"Jesus, is that why he killed his father? He didn't want him back with his mother? That's unbelievable."

"It's the way he was. And he didn't really know our father. Probably saw him as a stranger, and a threat."

# 66

I've been back a week with April now, and things have settled into a pattern.

It wasn't what I'd expected of married life. But it's not so bad.

I've got used to letting April make the decisions, and I might as well carry on that way. It saves a lot of arguments.

Looking at myself in the mirror, I'm in the best shape I've ever been in. Whether it's the steroids or the workouts, I don't care, if the results are there, and it's appreciated by April.

And by Dawn.

Although April doesn't want sex as much as I do, it balances out with having Dawn available from time to time.

I asked April the other day how she felt about me sleeping with Dawn, and she seemed surprised that I should ask. She said that as it was her sister, she knew she wasn't not going to try to steal me away. And it suited April, as then I didn't pester her so much for sex. She's right about that. After a session with Dawn, I need a week to recover.

Then there is the arrangement with Dawn and Robin. It's to be one week each month, with Dawn staying with April, and me with Robin. But it gives me an opportunity to go and see Karen once in a while, without April knowing. So although I grumble a little to April, the arrangement suits me fine.

So I have both April and Dawn available to me. Better than most guys get. And occasionally Karen, who's maybe the best of all.

Three beautiful women.

Looking in the mirror again, I couldn't help smile.

Robin would want to make it four.

# 67

~ ~ ~ ~ *April* ~ ~ ~ ~

I've told Grant that I'll be away tomorrow night. I'll be going to the theater with Scott, and then spending the night with him. Grant doesn't mind, as he'll have Dawn come to stay with him. He's oversexed, and that can be exciting when he makes love to me, as he's so physical. But it's quite stressful if I have it too often, so Dawn's a great safety valve.

Dawn wants to go to San Francisco again, but I'm holding out, as the longer I put it off, the more desperate she gets. When the time's right, I'll be able to trade it for another game with me as a dominatrix.

It was fun with Grant, and even better with her, but I want to do it with Robin next time. I think he'd make a good submissive. I mentioned it to her, and she refused, but if she wants the trip as much as I think she does, then she'll agree eventually.

She's suggested going to that gay club again, and getting the boys to have sex for us, but for now I'm not agreeing to any of it. Especially if it involves giving them drugs again.

I want to lead a normal life for a while.

\*     \*     \*

# Also by this author

## Mars Reversal

*Where Women Rule and Men Obey*

by Alex Rissini.

Utopia was the last place Greg wanted to be. A city where women rule and men are subordinate.

Yet Nicole had to go there for a one-month contract, and desperately wanted him to come with her. **And she was very persuasive.**

So, before long, they were in Utopia, with Greg then realizing that it was far worse than he'd anticipated. Still, it was only for one month.

**Until Nicole made a decision that would throw his life into turmoil …**

Greg then has to learn to conform to the laws and customs of Utopia, showing subservience to all women, and accepting Nicole's increasing dominance in their relationship. He reluctantly begins to accept it as his life from now on, with no chance of escape.

**But then things start happening that pose a far greater threat than before.**

And events make him increasingly nervous about the absolute power that Nicole has over him …

**Can there be any escape from the rule of women?**

Printed in Great Britain
by Amazon